PERFECT ALIBI
JANET HARWARD

Janet Harward lives in the West
Midlands with her husband and two
daughters. Her first novel, *Murder on The
English Riviera*, was published in 1995,
and was followed in by *The Teddy Bear
Murders*, the first Josephine Blake
mystery. She has since published *In
Memory of Murder,*, *Echoes of Death* and
Death is The Issue all featuring Josephine
Blake. *The Perfect Alibi* is the latest in the
Josephine Blake series.

D0433156

JANET HARWARD

PERFECT ALIBI

O'Neill Publishing

First published in Great Britain by O'Neill Publishing,
2000.

This edition 2000 O'Neill Publishing.

A CIP catalogue record for this book is
available from the British Library.

ISBN 0-9525161-5-2

9 8 7 6 5 4 3 2 1

Book design and Typography by DP Fact and Fiction.

Printed and bound in Great Britain by Omnia Books,
Glasgow.

PERFECT ALIBI

Chapter 1

THE CROWDS GATHERED in excitement on the large grassed area at the top of the cliff, waiting for the once in a lifetime experience.

How could a simple celestial show, produced by movements of the solar system, bring such a sense of wonder and magical anticipation to all who awaited the event?

What the people were about to encounter would burn brightly in their memory for the rest of their lives. They had come like true pilgrims; mothers, children, babes in arms, quasi druids, bikers and many more, to be part of something truly momentous.

Amongst the multitude stood a group of young female students from the local university, they were guzzling cans of lager and chatting as they waited for the big spectacular.

"It was good of your Mum to let us camp in her garden Sophie," one young woman said.

"Yeah, and to think we were going to trek all the way to St Ives," Miranda added.

"They reckon they're expecting rain down in Cornwall, and that we'll get a much better view," another one of the girls said.

The temperature started to drop and it became eerie and quiet as the birds stopped singing.

The looks of anticipation were similar on so many faces: excitement without fear, joy without explanation, with the expectation of something truly awesome coming in from the sea.

Sophie felt suddenly very cold and shivery. She had been suffering from flu for the past week, but was determined she would not miss the Total eclipse.

"You look terrible!" her friend noticed as she glanced her way.

"I'm fine, just cold."

"Here, take my jacket," Miranda said as she removed it without taking her eyes off the horizon.

It then became dark as the moon passed in front of the sun. There were shrieks of excitement and gasps of wonder as people looked up to the sky, seeing the real magic and endless mystery.

As it went black, it also went strangely quiet and hundreds of cameras flashed in futile wonderment. As the aurora came into view and shone like a diamond ring, the gasps and shouts of excitement became louder as the sun started to emerge from behind the moon. Many put on their protective glasses so they could continue to watch in safety.

Amidst the shouts of excitement and wonder came a piercing, terrifying scream. No-one paid attention to begin with, as there was so much commotion and noise, but it swiftly became a high-pitched, penetrating shriek that could be heard above the shouts of glee. Caught by the uniquely horrifying sound people finally stopped what they were doing and turned to the source of the commotion.

Miranda was on her knees by the side of Sophie, who was slumped on the ground face down with blood streaming down her back.

"Oh My God! She's dead. Christ, someone stabbed her, help me!" She screamed at the others, waving her blood drenched hands in the air.

* * *

"Well, was that it?" DS Bill Hughes asked as he shrugged his shoulders.

"Yes, bloody fantastic. Don't you think?" DI Josephine Blake replied without looking at him, as her eyes were firmly fixed skyward.

"A bit overrated in my opinion. I can't see what all the fuss was about, and to think two counties have had to draft all those extra police in to man the gigs and festivals, and I dread to think what the M5 will be like as people head home."

"Oh Bill, where's your sense of adventure? I felt like an excited child, you can be so cynical at times, you never get passionate or aroused by anything."

"That's a lie, when Torquay United scored in the last minute and equalised, I..."

Josephine interrupted his flow, "Well... yes... men do act like children once they get inside a football ground, I'll say that."

She turned to Bill, removing her dark glasses. "With all the TV coverage and hype before hand," Bill began, "I don't know what I was expecting, but it was certainly more than this, I found it a bit of an anti-climax."

"Well, we'll never see it again in this country, well not in our life-time anyway, but you could always travel to Australasia for the

12

next one in the year 2000, but since you're terrified of flying…" she said teasingly.

"Okay, don't rub it in. If we were meant to fly, we'd have wings," he replied.

"It's the safest form of travel," Josephine stated.

"Not in my book. Anyway, we're off duty in the next twenty minutes, fancy a drink?" he asked.

"Why not, sounds good to me!"

"Right, your round then, since you've had such a brilliant experience!" Bill smirked.

Just at that moment, his mobile phone rang. "Yes… you're joking… No, she's here with me now… whereabouts… right, we should be there in about half an hour, depending on the traffic."

He put his phone away looking miserable. "Why didn't I do the same as you and switch my mobile off?" he grunted.

"I only did it because I didn't want the damn thing ringing during the total eclipse," Josephine replied. "Nothing should spoil that magical moment."

"Well, it certainly wasn't magical for some poor sod, a young girl has been murdered on the cliff top at Berry Head in Brixham."

As they arrived twenty minutes or so later, there were still crowds of people about on this usually remote spot. No one seemed quite able to take in what had happened and that included the forensics and the police.

Sergeant Mike Rattigan was waiting a few yards from the scene to meet them.

"Right, fill me in," Josephine said.

"Well ma'am, the victim's name is Sophie Bryan, she was here with friends. One minute they were watching the eclipse, and the next thing, she was dead. We think she may have been stabbed, but there's no weapon. We'll have a clearer picture when the forensic pathologist arrives. The deceased's friends are sitting in a squad car, one is in a bit of a state, she's covered in blood and was hysterical when we arrived, but she seems to have calmed down a bit now," he informed them.

Josephine and Bill walked towards the scene of the crime where the police doctor was kneeling beside the body, which was lying face down. All they could see was a mass of long blonde hair and what appeared to be a lime green fleece jacket, although it was soaked in blood. The victim also wore jeans and trainers.

"I can't move her until Brian Morrison, the forensic pathologist gets here," the doctor informed them.

Josephine couldn't see the victim's face, when she did she always found it upsetting, despite attending many murder scenes over the years. "I'll go and talk to her friends in the car while I'm waiting for him to arrive," she told him.

As she opened the door of the police car there were two young girls sitting in the back seat and one in the front being comforted by a police woman.

"I'd like to speak to them," she told the WPC.

"Certainly, ma'am. Would you get out of the car?" she asked the girls.

"There's no need, I'll sit here and talk to them. Can you go and see if DS Hughes needs any assistance?" Josephine told her.

As she got into the car, she noticed the girls in the rear were smoking, and understandably they looked very nervous and agitated. The girl sitting next to her had white blonde hair, with a complexion to match, her face was expressionless, and she was in a state of shock.

"It was Miranda who saw her first," one of

the girls in the back told her. Josephine touched Miranda's hand; it was ice cold.

"Miranda," Josephine said gently. The girl didn't respond to begin with and just continued to stare ahead. Josephine realised how traumatised the girl must be, and was about to get one of the paramedics from a nearby ambulance to check her over, when the girl slowly turned her face towards Josephine. Josephine smiled gently, saying, "This must have been dreadful for you, but we need to know what happened before the body is removed," and gently slipped her arm around the girl's shoulder. Miranda suddenly burst into tears and sobbed, which Josephine considered a good sign, as she found it better for people in states of shock to let out their emotions.

After a few minutes, Miranda stopped crying and became more composed. "I couldn't believe it, one minute she was talking to me and then the next…"

"Had the total eclipse started?" Josephine enquired.

"Well yes… I think… I'm not sure," she started to become agitated again and was close to tears.

"Just take your time, and tell me what

happened as best you can," Josephine said kindly.

"Well, we were all excited, drinking and laughing you know, waiting for the big event. Then it went quiet and cold, so I gave Sophie my coat and we all watched the eclipse, it was such a wonderful sight... but now..."

She paused, unable to go on for a few moments. "As soon as the light returned, I went to say something to Sophie and there she was on the ground, with all that blood over her back..." She started to shake. "I'm sorry... I can't tell you anything else."

"Don't worry, we can always talk to you later, when you're feeling better you may remember more," Josephine turned to the two girls in the rear of the car. "I'll need to talk to you all so I'd like you to leave your names and addresses with the WPC, so we can contact you."

"We all live in a flat close to Exeter University," one told her. "Only we stayed at Sophie's house last night, her mum said we could stay for a couple of days."

"Oh my God," the other girl said, "Her parents, they don't know..."

"Leave that to us, we'll inform them. I suppose it might be best for you to collect any belongings from their house and go back home. I mean, they'll probably need to be alone," Josephine told them.

"We've got to get the tent," Miranda suddenly remembered. "Her parents have a guest house in Torquay, and they were fully booked with the eclipse and everything, so they said if the weather was fine, we could camp in their back garden. They're a great couple... so nice, and now they've lost Sophie," she uttered as her eyes filled with tears.

The other girls started to break down and cry. Despite being a professional, Josephine knew exactly how they were feeling. Being a mother herself, she had always felt terrible when she had to break news to parents that their children had been injured or murdered. It was a task that she'd had to perform many times in her career, and it never got any easier or less painful. Just at that moment, a knock came at the car window it was her sergeant, Bill Hughes. She opened the door.

"Brian Morrison is here now, he's examining the body."

"Right, thanks Bill. Listen girls, I think it's best if we go to see Sophie's parents before you all arrive back at their house." They all nodded in agreement. "So how about we get you back to the station where it's warm, and you can all have a hot drink and something to eat if you feel like it, and then you can give us a statement."

Just at that moment, the WPC returned and Josephine gave her instructions before making her way back to the crime scene with Bill.

Brian Morrison was a friend of Josephine's as well as a colleague, and he was always very sensitive to the situation in hand, unlike some forensic pathologists she had worked with in the past.

"She hasn't been dead any more than an hour or so," he informed them. "Because it's quite cold on this cliff, she was dressed in warm clothing."

"According to her friends, they believe she was killed during the actual eclipse, even though it only lasted about a minute or so."

Morrison glanced at his watch, it was ten minutes past midday. "Yes, I'd say that about fits in."

"Can you give us a cause of death?" Josephine asked.

"I'd say it's more than likely a stab wound, but I can tell you more after a thorough examination."

"The bastard! I suppose he or she waited until it went dark and then struck, you could say an ideal time to commit murder," Bill remarked.

"But a bit risky with all these people about surely," Josephine added.

"Yes, but maybe they were all so engrossed with this eclipse they never noticed anything," Bill suggested.

"That's true, everyone was so mesmerised and excited and maybe that's just what our murderer was banking on," she agreed.

"There might be more murders if that's the case, let's face it there are some sick weird bastards walking about."

"Don't say that Bill, this one is bad enough and we've got the terrible task of informing her parents and getting them to identify the body."

When the forensic team had taken all the photos they needed, both of the body and surrounding areas, Brian Morrison and his assistants carefully removed Sophie's body.

"I want the forensic team to take samples from the nearby grass and also I want the team of officers to speak to this crowd of people, it's possible they noticed something or someone acting suspiciously."

"I doubt it, they were all probably occupied by the event. It's unlikely they noticed anything except the bloody sun disappearing behind the moon," Bill remarked.

"Just look at them all," Josephine said, noticing the crowd that had not dispersed, but were standing behind the scene of crime tapes. "By the law of averages, one of them must have spotted something."

Chapter 2

MR AND MRS BRYAN were devastated on hearing the terrible news. Sophie's mother collapsed and her local GP had to be contacted to give her a strong sedative. Josephine decided now was not the time to question them, so she arranged to return the next day.

The following morning, Mrs Bryan was still in a deep sleep although her husband looked reasonably well under the circumstances. He had washed and dressed and was drinking coffee when Josephine and Bill arrived at the house. Mr Bryan was in his late fifties with greying hair. Josephine thought of him as the 'old school' type. It was obvious his daughter's death had devastated him, but he was putting a brave face on the situation, and trying to act as normally as possible under the circumstances, but Josephine knew that deep inside this poor man was destroyed.

"Would you like a coffee?" he asked. "I've just made some."

"No thank you Mr Bryan, but please drink yours," Josephine replied.

"I'm not thirsty, I just made it in the hope it might help keep me awake. I sat up all night thinking, you know how it is, breakfasts to make for the guests… although they've all left bar one couple and they are going home tomorrow. We've cancelled all our future bookings."

"That's quite understandable, you and Mrs Bryan need some time to yourselves," Josephine sympathised.

"Do we? Well yes, I suppose we do… It's just that when you are busy, there's no time to think."

His eyes filled with tears and he quickly wiped them away with his handkerchief, determined not to break down.

Oh, I wish he'd just let it all out and weep for his little girl, but I suppose he's trying to stay strong for his wife's sake, Josephine thought.

"I believe Sophie's friends were camping in your garden."

"Yes, she asked if they could stay but we hadn't got the room, these dates have been booked up for months because of the eclipse. They suggested camping and since the weather was fine and dry, and we've a big garden…" he said looking towards the window. "They brought their own tent, it was no problem to us."

24

"Was Sophie a student at Exeter University?" Bill asked.

"Well, she was doing a degree in fashion and design along with Miranda and Sally. The other girl, Trudy is studying Sociology I believe. Sophie had to struggle to get a place, as her A level results were not as good as she'd hoped for. Still, she got a place at university, but found the work too difficult and couldn't keep up. She asked us if we minded her jacking it in. I said of course not, as long as she was happy, that's all that mattered. Olive, my wife, didn't want her to leave, she'd boasted to all her friends how Sophie had got a place at Exeter, but I wasn't bothered. I was worried about her for the first couple of months as she was hanging about the house. But then she got a job as a trainee buyer with Debenhams and they were going to send her day release to college in September, she was really enjoying the job. In fact, she was just getting her life back together and doing what she wanted, and then this happened."

His eyes filled up with tears, Mr Bryan was a strong man, but he had just lost his only child. He slumped down on a chair and put his head in his hands and started to cry.

Josephine put her hand on his shoulder. "I'm sorry," he said looking up at her, "I'm so ashamed."

"Why, because you're crying? You've just lost your child, it's best to let these things out."

"No! I'm okay!" he said quickly wiping his eyes as he desperately tried to control his emotions.

Josephine wanted to put her arms around this man and mother him, even though he was a good ten years older than she was.

Oh I do wish you'd just let it all out. Cry an ocean of tears, sometimes it's the only way. Still if he's decided not to show his feelings especially in front of two relative strangers, I'll have to change the subject.

"So she still kept in touch with the girls?"

"Oh yes, all of them, especially Miranda. She's a very talented girl you know, designed some wonderful outfits. I think Sophie said something about her getting a place at London Fashion Week, apparently she was chosen out of about fifty others. Sophie would go to Exeter some weekends and stay with them at their flat. I think to begin with she regretted leaving, but since she'd started her new job, she was far more settled."

"I know this is painful for you to answer,"

Bill began, "but do you know of anyone who might want to harm your daughter, I mean were there any boyfriends on the scene?"

"No one, she was seeing a boy called Jason before she went to university, they kept in touch for the first couple of months or so, but then they sort of drifted apart, I think he's going out with someone else now," Mr Bryan informed him.

"And she hadn't met anyone since she'd returned home?" Bill continued.

"No, not to my knowledge, and Sophie was a very open girl, both with me and her mother, she wasn't the type to have any secrets. Everyone loved her; she didn't have any enemies. I can't think of any reason on this earth why anyone would want to kill her," he replied.

"Well, thank you for answering our questions. I know it's a very traumatic time for you. Perhaps in a day or so, I can come back to talk to your wife," Josephine said.

"Is there any need, she's in such a state?"

"I'm afraid we will still need to speak to her, there may be something she can tell us," Josephine replied.

"I doubt it, I've told you all I can."

"I know that Mr Bryan, but it's just normal

procedure. We'll be in touch and once again you have our deepest sympathies," Bill concluded.

As they left and walked down the path to the car, Mr Bryan slumped down on the settee and sobbed like a child.

As they were driving back in the car, Bill turned to Josephine and said, "I don't believe that about her having no boyfriends, let's face it she was a nice looking girl."

"Maybe she needed to get her mind straight and decide where she was going with her career when she came back home, and perhaps thought a relationship might interfere with that. Anyway, I'm sure she had a life at university that her parents probably knew nothing about, all girls have their secrets. We'll speak to all her friends in detail, they are bound to know more about both her private and social lives."

"Since she was killed during the eclipse, I think her murderer must have planned it sometime beforehand, and decided to strike as soon as it went dark. They'd got just a couple of minutes to approach her from behind, kill her and then disperse into the crowd of people," Bill suggested.

"Yes, that's sounds feasible, still we may know more when we go to the Forensic Pathology lab and see what else Brian Morrison can tell us."

* * *

They entered the morgue in their protective clothing and went to the table where the body lay. It was the first time they'd really had a good look at the victim's face. Sophie had been a pretty girl in life, with a pale freckled complexion and long blonde naturally curly hair.

"She just looks like Sleeping Beauty lying there," Josephine observed.

"I know, another wicked waste of life," Morrison sighed. "I'll tell you one thing, when Chloe gets older, I doubt if I'll ever let her out alone."

"We've both seen too much violence and devastation first hand, that's why it was so hard for me to let Jessica go. I was so protective, still at the end of the day, you've got to let them live their own lives and just hope and pray," Josephine replied.

"What can you tell us then Brian?" Bill asked a little impatiently.

"Twenty years of age, healthy female, height five foot five inches, weight nine stone two pounds, notice I've converted it for your benefit," Morrison told her as he knew Josephine could never get to grips with the metric system. "She wasn't a virgin, but that's quite usual for a girl of her age. Good teeth, no fillings, in fact she was in excellent health."

"That's no good to her now, is it?" Josephine said sadly, "Can you tell us anything about cause of death?"

"She was stabbed, the knife wound was in the middle of her back a few inches down from her shoulder blades and was so far penetrated, it punctured the heart. From the size of the cut, I'd say it was a smooth edged carving knife, definitely not serrated."

"Would death be instantaneous?" Josephine asked.

"Not quite, even though the knife pierced the edge of the heart, I would say she died after a minute or thereabout," Morrison replied.

"We'll have to get the area searched thoroughly. I suppose the killer may have dropped the weapon, or even thrown it over the cliff edge into the sea," Josephine suggested.

"Yes, but surely they would have to do that

while it was still dark, I mean carrying a knife dripping with blood, surely someone would have noticed something," Bill added.

"Unless they just hid the knife in a coat or whatever they were wearing at the time, in that case the killer must have been alone," Josephine said.

Bill looked at her a little vaguely, "What I mean is," she began to explain "there were lots of people in groups, friends, families all waiting for the eclipse, but the person we are looking for would most certainly be alone."

They turned their attention back to Brian Morrison. "Anything else you can tell us?" Josephine asked.

"Not at the moment, but I'll do more tests and examinations. The rough picture is, she was struck from behind, so obviously had no warning whatsoever. Unlike cases where the victims try to fight off their attackers, there are no signs of any skin or blood from her assailant, and since she died almost instantaneously, she couldn't grab at her assailant's clothing, so no chance of detecting any fibres."

"Could she have called for help?"

"I doubt it," Brian replied, "and anyway, would anyone have heard her with all the commotion?"

31

When they arrived back at the station, Bill lit a cigarette as he sat on the corner of Josephine's desk. "A perfect time to commit murder, everything goes dark with the eclipse, he pulls out the knife, and bingo, his job's done. Not much risk involved eh?"

"I'm not so sure Bill," Josephine said as she sipped her coffee. "It never went pitch black, and when she was struck her friends were standing by her, the killer must have taken some sort of a chance, that they wouldn't be noticed by someone in the crowd."

"Yes, but let's face it, they were all looking up at the eclipse. No one's going to bother what people are doing on the ground. The murderer could have come up close behind her. He would have had the knife concealed in a bag or underneath his coat. He's only going to produce it in the few seconds he ploughs it into her back. Then he puts it back in the bag, or hides it under his coat. All he has to do then is mingle with the crowds— he doesn't even have to run away!"

"I suppose he must have had some blood on him," Josephine said.

"Well not necessarily, just say he had been wearing a leather coat or something similar in thickness, if he put the knife into an inside pocket, even if it was soaked with blood, it wouldn't leak through to the hide."

"It's a pity Sophie wasn't wearing a leather coat, as it may have protected her, it would have been difficult to penetrate the leather before reaching the victim's skin," Josephine remarked.

"So can we assume the murderer would know how Sophie was going to be dressed beforehand, or say possibly have been stalking her," Bill suggested.

"It's possible," Josephine agreed, "but we know nothing much about the victim at the moment. We need to speak to her friends both here and at university, also her work colleagues and old boyfriends in the hope that something comes up."

"Anyway, I'm ravenous, fancy some lunch?"

"No thanks Bill, I'm on a diet."

"Well I don't know why. You haven't got a bad figure for your age, I for one like a woman who's a bit rounded."

"Do you know Bill, I don't know whether to take that as an insult or a compliment," she said before leaving.

After a few days' investigation, the information they had acquired about Sophie Bryan was that at the time of her death she had no boyfriend. She'd had a relationship with a boy at university, but since she had left it had fizzled out even though they said they would keep in touch.

From time to time she went out with a girl, Vanessa, who worked at the store, they would go to the cinema or out for an occasional drink. Vanessa said that as far as she was concerned Sophie had no enemies, and she could think of no one who would want to harm her. Even though they had statements from the girls present at Sophie's death, Josephine decided they needed to speak to them again and arranged to visit their flat in Exeter.

Josephine and Bill arrived at the flat where Miranda and Sally lived. It was a very large Victorian house converted into flats for students. It was painted in black and white and looked quite impressive from the outside. There were five wide concrete steps that led up to a solid oak front door with a large brass knocker. There were four push bells on the left-hand side of the door.

"Here we are, number 3A," Josephine said as she rang the bell.

As they waited on the steps Bill said, "I bet the landlord makes a bloody fortune. This is where the money is now—renting out property. So let's see, four flats and I reckon he must charge, what, say a hundred pound a week for each? That's four hundred pounds... er, let's see, one thousand six hundred pounds a month... not bad eh?"

"Yes, but he's got the upkeep remember," Josephine added.

"Even so, at the end of the day, you can always sell the property. If I came into any money that's what I'd do, take early retirement and invest it in rented properties."

"You sound very business-like all of a sudden. Have you switched from the Sunday Sport to the Financial Times now?" Josephine joked.

"Don't be ridiculous, I'd rather look at luscious ladies instead of the share index any day. It's just that you've got to think of your future. I mean, none of us are getting any younger, are we!"

Josephine was amazed. This was a serious side of Bill she, for one, had never seen before, and she was just about to answer, when a young girl wearing jeans and a ripped tee shirt answered the door.

She had short spiky hair, that was dyed a shade somewhere between purple and wine red and she wore a stud in her nose and was smoking a cigarette.

"Yeah, can I help you?"

"I'm DI Blake and this is DS Hughes, we've come to speak to Miranda and Sally," Josephine began.

"Oh... yeah... I remember her saying some coppers were coming, you'd better come up. We're on the third floor, do you think you can manage it?"

"I think we might just be able to," Josephine answered sarcastically.

As they followed the girl up the three flights of stairs, she appeared to be having more trouble than them as she was gasping and short of breath. "Perhaps you should give up the cigarettes, you sound a bit wheezy to me," Josephine remarked.

The girl tutted and mumbled something which they didn't quite catch, as she walked ahead of them into the room.

As they entered, Sally was standing on a chair wearing a black PVC dress, and Miranda was kneeling down, adjusting the hem. She turned round, "I won't keep you a moment, please have a seat."

After a minute or two had passed, Miranda stood up and stepped backwards as she looked at the girl on the chair, "Mmm... I think that's about it."

"That's a very unusual dress. In fact, I've never seen anything like it before," Josephine announced.

"Well, that's the idea, it's a collection I'm putting together for an interview I've got at a top design house, and it's got to look totally original," Miranda informed her.

"Well, it's certainly that! Not my taste, but I'm sure my daughter would adore it."

"Yes, well that's the age group I'm aiming for with my designs."

Just then, Sally got down off the chair. "I'll just go and change and I'll be with you," she said as she went out of the room.

As Josephine looked around, she could see this was very much a student's pad. It was very messy with posters on the walls and large cushions scattered on the floor. At the far end of the spacious lounge there was a large table that was covered in masses of cuttings, sketches, bits of fabric, pages torn out of magazines and lots of paraphernalia.

"I take it you're all doing a fashion and design degree," Josephine asked.

"Yes, all but Mo, who let you in, she's doing economics," Miranda informed her, "But I've just graduated, as I was in the year above the others."

"These aren't bad size flats," Bill noticed as he looked around the room.

"I don't suppose they are, but because two of us are studying fashion, we need so much space to do our pattern cutting," Miranda informed them.

Just at that moment Sally came back into the room, having changed into ski-pants and a baggy T-shirt.

"As you've probably gathered, we've come to ask you both some more questions about Sophie," Josephine started.

"I can't really see how we can help you anymore, we've told you everything we know," Miranda replied.

"At his moment in time, we can't seem to find any motive or reason for her murder," Bill told them.

"We were all shocked, I mean, I know it sounds a bit of a cliché, but everyone loved Sophie," Sally said.

"When she left the course, are you sure it

was because she couldn't cope with the work?" Josephine asked.

"Well, it wasn't that she couldn't cope, I believe she had a real talent for designing, it was putting the outfits together that Sophie hated, she never really got used to the industrial sewing machines. She'd always joke they were in charge of her instead of the other way round," Sally's eyes began to fill up, "God… I do miss her."

"We all do Sally, but it's not going to bring her back is it?" Miranda said, a little too sharply Josephine thought, considering they were talking about their dead friend.

"The only thing we can do for Sophie now is find her killer, and that's why we need your help," Josephine continued.

"If I could think of anything that would nail the son of a bitch who murdered her, don't you think I'd tell you?" Miranda snapped.

"We've exhausted all the possibilities of people she knew at home in Torquay. So the only thing we have left is her life here. So you reckon she had no regrets giving up the course?" Josephine asked.

"I think she was a little unsure to start with that she was doing the right thing, but since she started her new job, she was far more settled, when she came down to stay with us, she said how much she was enjoying it."

Mmm, I wonder if she just told you that because she didn't want to appear a failure, Josephine thought to herself.

"So she had no enemies, no one on the course, tutors, students, are you sure she hadn't ruffled anyone's feathers, or got on the wrong side of anybody?" Bill suggested.

"Apart from the tutors, who we all hate and despise, you mean," Miranda replied jokingly.

"What do you mean?" Bill asked.

"Well, let's face it, they are all frustrated designers who could never make it in the fashion world, so they had to settle for jobs as lecturers instead."

"Well, I certainly wouldn't call that a failure. In fact, I'd say to become a university lecturer is making a success of your life," Josephine remarked.

"Not if you are a designer, the ultimate goal is to see your creations on the catwalk or get a job designing for some famous fashion house," Miranda replied.

"Yes, but how many people really achieve that? There are so many people we know who have just wasted their degrees," Sally intervened.

"That's true, but I intend to make it to the top no matter what it takes," Miranda announced in a firm voice.

Yes, I really believe you do Josephine thought as she looked at the grit and determination in her face.

"What about boyfriends, was there anyone special?" Bill enquired.

"There were one or two blokes on our course, but they were just friends," Miranda replied.

"What about Robin?" Sally said.

"That was over two months ago," Miranda stated.

"Yes, but he did give Sophie a bit of grief, if you remember," Sally continued.

"No more so than any of us get if we are dumb enough to put up with it."

The two girls were having a conversation between themselves, which annoyed Josephine a little. "Do you mind filling me in on this, what's his name, Robin?"

"There's nothing much to tell," Miranda said shrugging her shoulders.

"Let me be the judge of that," Josephine told her.

"Well, it's just that Robin and Sophie went out together for a short time, but Sophie thought he was a bit strange, so she finished with him. There was no sweat as they'd only been seeing one another a few weeks, she was glad to be rid of him," Miranda informed them.

"But he didn't feel the same," Sally interrupted, "He kept phoning her up and waiting for her after lectures, pestering her to go back out with him."

"Was Sophie afraid of him?" Josephine asked.

"Oh no," Miranda said, "She wouldn't let a boy get to her, she'd got more sense than that."

"It sounds to me like he was stalking her, and she may have been more bothered than she was prepared to admit," Josephine said.

"She got it sorted anyway. They went out for a quiet drink together one evening, and Sophie told him she only thought of him as a friend and there could never be anything more than that between them."

"Did he accept this?" Bill asked.

"Well yes... he seemed to," Sally began, "Never really bothered again."

"I'm sure you're barking up the wrong tree. You are mistaken if you think he had anything to do with her death," Miranda told them.

Josephine looked over at her thinking what an obnoxious and over confident young woman she was.

"You might know a lot about fashion and design, but how you can think you know the first thing about police work amazes me," Josephine began. Miranda looked slightly taken aback. "Sophie may have given you the impression she wasn't bothered by his unwanted attentions, but it could have affected her far more than she was letting on, and we don't know for certain that this Robin accepted her rejection. So whether we're 'barking up the wrong tree', as you put it, is not an issue. No one really knows what's going on in other people's minds."

"Do you have Robin's address?" Bill asked them.

"No, but I can tell you what course he's on, and the admin. at the university can give you the details," Sally told him.

Bill got out his notepad and pen and took down the relevant information.

"Right, we'll be in touch. If you can think of anything else that might be of help please contact us," Josephine said as she handed over her card before leaving.

Robin Steadwell lived in the university's halls of residence, and they arranged to speak to him in his room at four-thirty after his last lecture.

He seemed a very pleasant young man; he had sandy hair, freckles, and a nice smile, and didn't seem capable of harming a fly. But Josephine knew only too well how deceptive appearances could be, although she always trusted her own intuition.

Apparently he knew of Sophie's tragic death even though he hadn't seen her for some time, her murder was common knowledge in the university. He appeared genuinely upset and shocked.

"I'm told that you went out with Sophie for a while," Josephine began.

"That's right, it was a few weeks," he replied.

"So what happened?" Bill continued.

"We decided we weren't really that suited and just became friends," he stated.

"Isn't it true that she finished with you, but you couldn't accept it, and were bombarding her with phone calls, and waiting for her after lectures?" Josephine asked.

"Well... I may have..."

"Do you realise stalking is now a major crime?"

"Now look here, I wasn't stalking her…" he became red in the face, "I only wanted her to see sense," he put his head in his hands and his eyes filled with tears. "I really thought a lot of Sophie," he uttered.

"Then I suggest, for your own good, and to help us find who murdered her you tell us all you can," Bill told him.

"Okay, I always liked Sophie and when she agreed to go out with me, I thought it was great. We went out a few times, but I was a bit shy and never spoke much, I think she got fed up, because she told me one night she didn't think it was working out. The reason I kept phoning was because I wanted to tell her I was sorry for being a bore, and it was only because I was so shy. I desperately needed another chance. She finally agreed to see me for a quick drink in the student bar, and I told her just how I felt. She said she just wanted us to be friends, and I sort of knew by the look on her face, we could never be anything else and I accepted it."

"So it wasn't a case of 'if I can't have her nobody else will'?" Bill suggested.

"No way! I wouldn't harm Sophie, I just wanted to take care of her!" He stood up shaking and his face was flushed.

"Do you know of anyone who would want to harm her?" Josephine asked.

"No... she was lovely... I just can't imagine..."

"Can you tell us of your whereabouts on Wednesday the eleventh of August?"

"Oh God, is that when she was killed?" Robin asked.

"Yes, didn't you know it was during the total eclipse that Sophie was stabbed?"

"There have been so many different stories going around, I didn't know exactly what happened. I was camping in France at the time of the total eclipse with a group of friends."

He had just told them he'd got an alibi, but didn't seem to realise that fact.

"We will need all the details and names of the people you travelled with," Bill told him.

"That won't be a problem," he replied.

"If they check out, you'll be in the clear, so you will have nothing to worry about," Josephine told him thinking he would be relieved that he wasn't a suspect.

"It won't bring Sophie back though, will it?" he said emotionally.

A day or so later when Josephine's team confirmed the details, everything Robin

Steadwell had told them checked out. He had taken the Euro Tunnel train with a group of friends on Saturday the seventh of August and returned on the following Saturday which was the fourteenth.

They looked into the remote possibility that he could have somehow returned to Britain without the others knowing, but on the day of the eclipse he was at a restaurant with friends, he had a cast iron alibi.

Chapter 3

JOSEPHINE POURED HERSELF a glass of wine as she sat on her veranda looking out to sea. It was a warm sunny day, and there was still one week left in August. Babbacombe was still relatively busy with holidaymakers, even though it wasn't as bustling as Torquay. They still had the bank holiday weekend to come.

She had been so tied up with the case in hand that she hadn't had time to miss her daughter Jessica who was working in Greece with a group of friends.

Andrew Blythe who she affectionately referred to as her 'other half' had been working in London for the past six weeks. He was a forensic psychologist who Josephine had been with for almost two years, since her divorce. When in a serious mood, she would refer to him as 'her Saviour', as he had restored her confidence and faith in men after she had parted from her husband Tom. But more importantly, Andrew had saved her life a year previous, when she was being viciously attacked by a knife wielding serial killer who seemed to think he was a reincarnation of Jack the Ripper!

She sat back in her deck chair feeling the warm sun on her face, and started to doze for a few minutes, when suddenly the phone rang. She jumped up, slightly dazed, and went into the lounge to answer it.

"Are you okay?"

"Who's that?"

"It's Bill. What's the matter, can't you recognise my voice?"

"I was asleep," she replied a little disorientated.

"I thought I might pop over, there's a few things I want to go through with you about the case."

"Have you eaten?" Josephine asked.

"Come to think of it, no, but I'm sure you'll rustle something up with your culinary skills."

"So you'd like to see me slaving over a hot stove on a day like today," she joked.

"No... just pop one of them pepperoni pizzas that Jessica's always buying in the oven, you've got loads in your freezer...I'll bring some beers..."

He hung up before Josephine had any chance to answer.

Dear Bill, he never changes! she thought as she

went back out onto the veranda to finish her wine.

She'd worked with him for the last five years, and he was so much a part of her, she couldn't imagine life without him. Although they had never been anything more than just good friends.

In the early days of their working relationship, Bill had been a bit of a chauvinist but Josephine had soon changed him. He had been divorced for three years, and had never really found the right woman to replace his wife, whom he missed more than he cared to admit.

Thirty minutes or so later, the bell rang and Josephine answered the door. "You didn't say we were having a party," she said looking at the large box of lagers that Bill was cradling in his arms.

He followed her through to the kitchen and opened a can, before stacking the others in her fridge. "Want one?" he offered.

"No thanks, I'm drinking wine. I thought we'd have lunch on the balcony it's such a lovely day," she suggested.

"That sounds great," Bill said as he followed her outside.

The table was all laid. Josephine had

prepared two tuna fish salads and opened a bottle of chilled wine.

"Where's the pizza?" he asked. "I fancied something hot."

"In this weather? Anyway, you need to lose weight, and this will do you good. You know Bill, you're a perfect candidate for a heart attack," she said looking at his rather ample stomach. "You should exercise more."

"My God! It's like being married again, I'm fine as I am."

"I don't agree, you need to take more care of yourself Bill."

"I've never failed a police medical," he declared proudly.

"There's always a first time," she told him.

After they had eaten their salad, Bill sat back in his chair and lit a cigarette. "You don't mind?" he asked.

"No, you can smoke out here. It's just that now I've given up I don't like smoke in the house."

"I must admit," he said reaching for his beer "I enjoyed that salad more than I thought I would."

"Your stomach just needs educating," Josephine said smiling.

"How's Andrew?"

"Fine, he phoned last night, he's asked me to marry him," Josephine disclosed.

"That's great, congratulations!" Bill said holding up his glass in the way of a toast.

"Don't jump the gun, I haven't accepted yet."

"Why ever not? He's a good bloke, old Andrew," Bill stated.

"You never used to feel that way," Josephine reminded him.

"Okay, I agree, I had my doubts about him in the early days, but I've grown to like him, and let's face it, how many men would put their life on the line for a woman?"

"Tom and I have only been divorced just over eighteen months. I don't know whether I want to take the plunge again, after one failed marriage."

"You and Tom had a good marriage. It lasted twenty years, I wouldn't exactly call that a failure."

"No, perhaps you're right. Oh, I don't know Bill… I do love Andrew," she sighed.

"None of us are getting any younger, and if you don't snap him up then maybe no one else will have you. I mean you're not bad for your age, but let's face it, you're no spring chicken."

"That's what I like about you. You really give a girl confidence," she said playfully poking him in the stomach. "Anyway," she said pushing her fingers through her short blonde hair, "I need to talk about this case, that is, while I've still got my own teeth and faculties."

Secretly Bill still thought Josephine an attractive woman, but he would never tell her so. She was almost forty-eight and still had a slender figure, despite the fact she had put on a few pounds recently. She had lines beneath her bright blue eyes and there were a few grey hairs creeping through the blonde.

"As you know," Bill began, "Steadwell's alibi checked out completely."

"I never really suspected him anyway, he didn't look the type," she said.

"So where do we go from here? There doesn't seem to be any possible motive even though we have delved into her life with her family, friends and working colleagues."

"We could go back to Brian Morrison and see if he has found anything else about her assailant, although I'm not very optimistic. He's so thorough in his work, I doubt there's anything he's overlooked," Josephine told him.

"Her parents keep asking when they can have the body, for the funeral arrangements. So we're going to have to give the Chief a good reason why we need to keep it any longer," Bill remarked.

"I know it sounds like a cliché, but she really did seem to be the girl that everybody loved. If there is some sinister reason for her death, I'm damned if I can figure out what it could be. Maybe I'm losing my touch."

"There is one other thing we haven't looked into," Bill told her.

"What's that?"

"Well, she was murdered during the total eclipse, right... some might say an ideal time to strike, a guaranteed minute or so of darkness," Bill began.

"Yes, but the killer was still taking a chance, Sophie was surrounded by people, although they were engrossed in the eclipse."

"Okay, just let me run this past you," Bill started. "Let's say he or she is some sort of madman who has to strike at that particular time. I don't know... perhaps it's some pagan ritual, and poor Sophie was in the wrong place at the wrong time. The killer may have just picked her out of the crowd at random, like picking a card out of a pack," Bill suggested.

"So what if she moved away in front of a friend?" Josephine said.

"Then perhaps, some other poor sod would have a knife through their back... I don't know."

"I think it's worth looking into..." she sounded doubtful.

"You sound a little vague..." Bill said.

"Oh, I don't know Bill. Despite the fact we had that copycat Jack the Ripper killer, I'm not really into these occult things, I like the good old-fashioned motive, where A needs B out of the way for some specific reason. Still, since there's nothing else left to go on, I suppose we've no alternative."

Chapter 4

JOSEPHINE AND BILL had made certain enquiries, and come up with the name of a Professor Edwin Waltham, who was a renowned astronomer who worked at Plymouth University, so they made an appointment to speak to him.

As Bill drove down the motorway towards their destination he turned his head to look at Josephine.

"Bill, please don't take your eyes off the road," she said tersely.

"Okay, don't panic," he said as he turned back and focussed on the road ahead.

"You know how much I hate these motorways at the best of times, but in the holiday season…" she began.

"Well, I'm the one who's driving, so I don't know what you're getting all het up about."

"It's worse for me, when I'm not behind the wheel I don't feel in control," she told Bill.

"We can always pull in at the next exit if you want to take over," Bill offered, knowing full well that Josephine would refuse.

"No, you carry on, just concentrate on the road."

"I'll have you know, I'm an excellent driver," Bill boasted.

"It's not you I'm worried about, it's these other lunatics," Josephine uttered as a lorry went hurtling past them into the outside lane.

"Now that's what pisses me off. Why those bloody big things can't stop in their own lane I don't know. Anyway, what I was going to say..." he continued making sure he didn't turn to look at Josephine. "Even though this was originally my suggestion, I don't really hold with these astrologer chaps, I mean as if you can predict things by the stars and someone's birth date..."

"We are going to see an astronomer Bill, there's a big difference," Josephine corrected him. "Astrology is the study of possible influence of the stars on human events, so you have your so called fortune tellers etc. If you called Professor Waltham an astrologer, I don't think he'd be too pleased. Astronomy is the study of planets and stars."

"I bet he's just like Patrick Moore, a real old professor type," Bill remarked taking one hand off the wheel and reaching for a cigarette.

"Don't you dare try and light that while you're driving, you'll have us killed…" Josephine said. "I'll do it for you."

Some thirty minutes or so later they were being taken to Professor Edwin Waltham's office. As they entered he was sitting behind a rather grand looking mahogany desk. He stood up and held out his hand to welcome them.

"I'm DI Blake and this is DS Hughes, I believe one of my sergeants spoke to you on the phone."

"Yes of course, please take a seat," he told them.

Professor Waltham was nothing like Patrick Moore in any way. He couldn't have been much more than fifty and had brown eyes and dark hair, that was just starting to turn grey slightly at the temples, his skin was tanned, and Josephine thought him a very attractive man.

"Just before we begin, I'll get Penny to bring us some refreshments. Tea, coffee, or would you prefer something cool…?" he asked them.

"Something cool would be nice," Josephine replied.

He got up and opened his office door and said to the young woman in the adjoining office, "Can we have three glasses of lemon cordial, Penny?"

When he returned to his desk he began, "Now, I believe you are making enquiries about someone who was murdered during the total eclipse."

"Yes that's right. We cannot find any possible motive and have no suspects, so we thought could it be some sort of ritual killing, if that doesn't sound too far-fetched," Josephine replied.

"Not at all," he said smiling at her. "Now before I begin, let me make one thing clear, although I do not wish to insult your intelligence in any way. Some people confuse me with an astrologer, which is rather annoying as you may appreciate. I am a professor of astronomy which is a comprehensive study and analysis of the planets and stars, their movements, and relative positions and compositions."

It was almost as if he knew of their conversation during the journey. "Yes, we are fully aware of that professor," Bill lied.

"Can you tell us about a solar eclipse," Josephine asked.

"With pleasure, it's one of the many things that excites me. A total eclipse of the sun," he began, "is one of the most spectacular phenomena in nature, so rare and beautiful that astronomers will travel across the world to see one. I myself went to Russia in 1997 to see a total eclipse of the sun on March the ninth; it lasted two minutes and fifty seconds. There is one due on the twenty-first of June 2001 in Central Africa, which will last for five minutes, and I hope to see that one also."

Why anyone would want to travel to the other side of the earth just to see everything go black was a complete mystery to Bill, but then so many thing were.

"What exactly happens?" Josephine asked.

"It begins as the moon glides across the sun's face and it almost looks as if it's taking a bite out of the sun. In fact, the ancient Chinese believed eclipses were caused by a dragon attempting to devour the sun, and they banged gongs to frighten the creature away, a technique that rarely failed. The eclipse progresses slowly until the sky becomes dark. Birds and animals, fooled by the deepening twilight, bed down for the night. Finally, only a thin crescent of sunlight remains, which for the last few seconds is broken up into a necklace of brilliant points like mountain peaks along the moon's edge. This effect is known as 'Bailey's Beads', after the English astronomer Francis Bailey, who described it at an eclipse in 1836. Often one bead shines more brightly than the others which is called the 'Diamond Ring Effect'."

"I'm no authority, but I was absolutely thrilled by the recent total eclipse," Josephine told the professor. She was in awe of his immense knowledge. "I should imagine it's a fascinating subject to study."

"I've always thought so," he replied smiling.

Just at that moment, his secretary knocked at the door and she placed three glasses of iced cordial on the table.

"I needed this," Bill said reaching for his glass, *Shame it's not lager though,* he thought.

After taking a sip from his glass, the Professor continued, "A total eclipse brings into view the sun's corona. A faint halo of gases whose pearly light is normally swamped by the brilliance of the sun's disc. Totality can last from a few seconds up to seven and a half minutes, although the usual duration is two or three minutes. The moon moves off the face of the sun like a curtain being drawn back, and the grand spectacle is over."

Josephine sighed inwardly. Professor Waltham was such a good talker, and described the events with so much passion that she felt like a disappointed child whose bedtime story had just ended. Bill, on the other hand, was getting bored with his lesson in astronomy.

"What we'd like to know, Professor, is are there superstitions and rituals attached to the event?" he asked.

"Eclipses have terrified mankind until quite recent times, and given rise to numerous superstitions," he began to explain, "the old idea was that when darkness fell across the face of the sun, disaster was imminent, which has now proved incorrect, as we know, eclipses cause such events. At the same time, the moon has been held in awe for centuries, some claim a full moon can turn people mad. The word 'lunatic' is derived from the Latin word for moon 'luna'."

"But can the eclipse cause people to kill?" Josephine asked.

"I'm no psychologist, but it has been thought that evil spirits are robbing the earth of light. Eclipses have been often interpreted as omens of death of some high-ranking person. The Roman Emperor Nero died close to an eclipse, and Catherine of Aragon, first wife of Henry the Eighth, died close to an eclipse in 1536," he enlightened them.

"They believed they would bring some great calamity to the earth, such as the Black Death in 1348, and the outbreak of the First World War in 1914. Many people believed the world would end during an eclipse. I think it could certainly affect personality and it's quite possible someone might have a malevolent idea that they needed to take a life during the eclipse. Even though I have a scientific mind, I understand that these things can happen."

"I do agree with what you've said, although it's possible our killer may have been unhinged to begin with," Josephine told him. She could have sat all day, listening to him, as she found him fascinating, but Bill said, "Well thank you so much, Professor Waltham, it was very interesting."

"Yes, it was good of you to spare us the time," Josephine added as she stood up from her chair.

"I suppose it's rather sad if some lunatic did take the poor girl's life, just because of some pagan belief," he sighed.

"Well, until we can find a feasible motive, which we don't have at present, it's all we have left to go on," Josephine told him.

As they were making their way back to the car, Bill turned to Josephine, "He certainly wasn't what I was expecting, not your fuddy duddy, professor type at all, but he knew his stuff."

"Yes... he was a fascinating man," Josephine sighed.

"I can see now why you can't make your mind up about marrying Andrew."

"What do you mean?" she snapped.

"You've got a wandering eye," Bill teased.

"I found him a very attractive and intelligent man, and that's as far as it goes," she stated.

"Yes, but would you kick him out of bed?" he asked her.

"Bill, you're incorrigible!!"

The following day Josephine had the team assembled in the incident room. She told them, "We don't seem to be progressing the way we would have liked with this case. After extensive interviews with Sophie Bryan's friends, family and colleagues, we cannot find one person who had a reason to want her dead. Now, I realise," she continued, "it's possible someone may be lying or holding back information, but everyone we've spoken to has said the same about Sophie, she didn't have an enemy in the world. For a short time we did think Robin Steadwell, an old boyfriend, might have been implicated, but it turns out he had an alibi. Now DS Hughes believes it may be some sort of pagan or ritual killing. I know these people usually work in groups, but it's possible it's some crazed lunatic who needed to kill during the eclipse."

Bill Hughes stood up and began, "The DI and myself visited a Professor Waltham, who is an expert in astronomy, he gave us not just information about the eclipse itself, but also the myths and superstitions that are linked to it. We believe it's possible some madman who didn't even know Sophie may have just picked her out of the crowd."

"How are the investigations going into the people that were there at the time?" Josephine asked DC Barnes.

"No-one can recall seeing anyone acting strangely or suspiciously. Still, I suppose it was because they were all engrossed in the eclipse," he replied.

"If you think about it there are only two possibilities for this crime," Josephine began. "Either it was a premeditated planned murder that the murderer had worked out to the last detail, or it was just some crazed killer who decided for some reason that he or she had to take a life at the time of the eclipse. But we have nothing concrete to support either theory."

Chapter 5

One Month Later

SOME WOULD CALL the flat that Jack and Gary shared a typical 'bachelor's pad', if that term is really appropriate in today's world, where both sexes are regarded as equal. The so-called 'woman's touch', a vase of fresh flowers, a pretty cushion or bedspread seemed to be becoming a thing of the past. In fact, with many of the modern day clothes, jeans, jumpers and trousers being unisex, probably only certain items of make-up or perfume could determine which sex occupied a certain abode, and that was sometimes debatable.

However, in Jack and Gary's case, the posters of rather well-endowed naked women that adorned the walls, and the soft porn magazines beneath the coffee table, left no-one in any doubt that this was the abode of two hot blooded males!

They were lolling on the floor in front of the gas fire listening to a Bob Marley CD, and not doing the connoisseur brandy justice, by drinking it out of two cracked mugs, and munching a bag of stale tortillas they had found in the kitchen cupboard.

They usually drank the cheapest brand of supermarket lager they could find, but Jack's mother had brought him two bottles of good quality brandy back from a recent trip to Spain, along with four hundred cigarettes. It was, according to her, to be kept for 'medicinal purposes only, if they had a cold or flu'.

But at the rate they were knocking it back there would be nothing left by the end of the night.

"Your turn," Jack said, as the doorbell rang. Gary got up to let Rob in.

"I see you've started without me," he said reaching for the packet of cigarettes that lay on the table.

"Don't worry, there's plenty left," Jack told him holding up a half full bottle of brandy.

They sat and drank, smoked and chatted. "What more could you want in life?" Gary said "Good friends, fine brandy, and plenty of fags."

"A balti curry with rice and naan," Rob suggested.

"Are you offering to treat us?" Gary asked.

"Don't be daft, I'm skint, bloody starving though," Rob told him.

"I can't help you I'm afraid. There's nothing in the fridge, not even a slice of bread."

They continued to drink the brandy and chat. They spoke about everything these three friends. Their families, past girlfriends, their hopes and fears, even who they were having sex with, and what she was like, as they became more and more inebriated.

"I love all women," Gary announced in a befuddled manner. "And men too, but not in the same way you understand."

"What about you Jack?" he asked slurring his words slightly.

"Yeah, all but one," Jack answered with a glare in his eyes.

"I hope you're not referring to your mum, 'cause in my opinion she's a real doll!" Rob said looking at the two empty bottles of brandy and the cigarettes that lay on the table.

"Don't be daft, it's that cow who pinched all my designs, and sent them off to London as her own," Jack said angrily. "I stayed up night after night, trying to get it just right. I sweated blood and tears creating them, they were original, it's almost like she's raped my mind."

"You should have had it out with her there and then," Gary said.

71

"I did, but she just denied it. I had an almighty row with her in front of several people. Still, she may have passed my work off as her own, but she'll never be able to repeat it."

"She's not a bad fashion designer though," Gary observed.

"Middle of the road in my opinion. She hasn't got that certain flare to make it, that's why Miranda ripped off my ideas. She won the competition with my bloody work!"

"Yes, but they only paid her two hundred pounds," Gary replied.

"It wasn't the money you bloody fool, it was the fact that the prize was also three months' work experience in a top fashion house in London. That's far more important than two hundred bloody quid, but I don't expect you to realise that."

Gary's mind went back to that Saturday evening several months previously, when Jack had gone home for the weekend. Miranda had arrived on the pretence that she needed to talk to Jack about a project they were working on. Looking back, Gary now realised she must have known he would be out. There was no doubt, the sex was brilliant, she was good in bed, but she was only there to steal Jack's designs. She had used Gary and it hurt. When he asked her out for a drink a few days later, she had completely shunned him. It wasn't until a week or so later, when Jack's designs were missing, that Gary realised Miranda had planned it all beforehand.

He'd never told Jack what happened that night, because he felt so guilty, even though he had no idea what Miranda was up to. He decided now was the time to come clean and get it off his chest.

"Listen Jack, she came round one night when you were away, and we ended up sleeping together. I had no idea she was going to pinch your designs, in fact I don't even know how she got into your bedroom. There was me thinking she fancied me, and all the time... I feel really bad Jack, I hadn't the slightest inkling..."

"Don't worry Gary, you weren't to know. It's just the sort of thing that evil bitch would do. Perhaps I should have kept them locked away somewhere. I didn't anticipate the lengths she would go to," Jack told him.

"I feel such a shit, if only I'd known what she was up to..." Gary said dismally.

"She's a devious bastard! No one could tell what she had up her sleeve. It's months ago now, but I'll never forget or forgive, somehow I'll get my revenge!"

Gary was relieved that Jack didn't really blame him. They were such good mates, but Jack was so obsessed with his work, he really did think he'd never forgive him.

"I have no grudge against you, but I tell you something, if I could have one person dead, it would be her," Jack said, knocking back the remains of his brandy.

Gary looked shocked. *It must be the drink talking, he doesn't know what he's saying*, he thought.

It was as if Jack had read his mind. "And it's not because I'm drunk, I could easily kill her with no remorse whatsoever."

"Then why don't you?" Rob asked him.

"Because, I've threatened her in public. I'd be the first person the police would come looking for if dear Miranda were to snuff it, the prime suspect."

"I don't know how you could say that," Gary remarked.

"Why not?" Rob intervened, "Surely, there's someone you'd like to see dead."

"No... no one," Gary replied.

He suddenly thought of his sister; Isabella had been so alive and vibrant, with a mass of shiny black hair just like his mother's. Since her death, it was the only thing he really could recall, apart from when they were small and would make mud pies in the sand pit at the bottom of the garden. He would never forget that cute face, smeared in mud. Being the elder, he would always get the blame, but it never bothered him. They had fought from time to time like all brothers and sisters, but he had loved her so much and now she was gone.

His reminiscing was interrupted when Rob said, "Well I could easily kill old Ramsey for what he did to Claire. I hold him totally responsible for her death."

"But she took a drugs overdose," Gary said, he was loathe to say the word suicide.

"Claire did it deliberately, she intended to kill herself," Rob told him. "Ramsey told Claire her work was useless and she'd never make it as a scientist, and that she was wasting her time."

"Yes, but how many times have the tutors told us that, if we believed everything they said we'd all top ourselves," Gary replied.

Rob stood up angrily; he looked as if he was about to hit Gary.

"Don't get me wrong, I liked Claire, I know

Ramsey was a shit, but perhaps she took it all a bit too personal, and let's face it Rob, I know you loved her, but she did have a drugs problem."

"I'm not denying that, but she was getting help and coming off them slowly. Her prescription had been cut down quite a bit," Rob began. "You may think I was kidding myself, but I'm convinced, with my help, she would have eventually kicked the habit. But Ramsey gave her so much stress, she'd started injecting herself again. Even I'm not completely sure whether the overdose was intentional or an accident, but whatever it was it was Ramsey's fault."

"Well, you knew her better than anyone Rob, so you can make the best judgement, but perhaps you were too involved," Jack observed.

"Listen Jack," he said lighting another cigarette, "you don't know the nights I spent with her crying, about how he'd ridiculed her in front of the entire class, he constantly put her down."

"Then I don't know why you didn't go and sort him out. If it was my girl, I'd have punched his bloody head in," Jack stated.

"Don't you think I wanted to, but Claire

begged me not to say anything, she said it would only make matters worse. But I did have that set to with him just before Claire's funeral if you remember. I pushed him up against the wall and broke his arm. I wish it had been his bloody neck," Rob said bitterly.

"You were lucky he didn't report you to the police," Gary said.

"I think he knew he had it coming after what he'd done to Claire. Still, as you said Jack, if old Ramsey was found floating face down in the river, I'd be the prime suspect. Everyone knows I hated him, as I'd threatened him so many times."

"So come on, what about you?" Jack said looking at Gary.

"What about me?" Gary asked.

"Who would you like to murder?" Jack continued.

"No one... I've told you that already... I mean there are people I don't like, most I'd like to see the back of... but kill someone... no way," he replied.

Since Rob, like the rest of them had consumed far too much brandy, he decided to crash down on the sofa, for what was left of the morning, as it was after 3 a.m. before Jack and Gary retired.

"God I'm beat, and I've got all those designs to do tomorrow, I hope Mac's in a good mood," Jack said as he closed his bedroom door.

Gary was exhausted, but he didn't get the good night's sleep he'd hoped he would.

Flashes of Isabella, his sister, kept coming to his mind as he tried to doze; his night was fraught with dreams of her death and funeral.

The next morning at eight-thirty, he dragged himself into the kitchen. "God, I feel like shit. All that drink on an empty stomach!"

He opened the fridge door in search of food, forgetting they hadn't got a thing in. "My throat's as dry as sand," Gary said rubbing his neck.

"Here, drink this," Jack said placing a mug of black coffee in front of Gary.

"I see Rob's still dead to the world," Gary noticed as his friend lay snoring on the settee.

"Yes—I'll pop downstairs to see if the girls in the flat below have got anything we can have for breakfast," Jack said running his fingers through his long black hair.

He returned some minutes later with a

bottle of milk and half a loaf of bread. "No butter I'm afraid, still dry toast is better than nothing I suppose."

"I've got to dash anyway, forget about my toast," Gary said mooching through the kitchen cupboards. "Any paracetamol? My head's splitting."

"There's some in the bathroom I think," Jack said.

After Gary had found the tablets and taken two, he picked up a slice of dry toast from the kitchen table and left. "See you later," he shouted slamming the front door.

Just before Jack was leaving he poked Rob on the shoulder. "You'd better get up, I'm going now."

"Eh... what... What time is it?" Rob muttered in a daze.

"Ten o'clock, get moving," Jack shouted.

After showering and making himself a black coffee, Rob started to feel almost human again, although his head was pounding. He suddenly realised he was doing the morning shift at the local pub where he worked and was due in at eleven thirty; he glanced at the clock on the kitchen wall, it was eleven-fourteen, and he thought he may just make it if he ran all the way there.

The phone in the flat began to ring, and Rob ignored it to begin with. "It can't be for me anyway," he thought, and was just about to go out of the door when he decided to answer it.

"Yes," he said impatiently.

"Gary, is that you?" A man's voice spoke urgently.

"No, he's gone to college," Rob told him.

"Is that Jack," the voice demanded.

"No, he's not here either, I'm Rob, a friend of theirs."

"It's vital I contact Gary at once, it's an emergency!"

"I can give you the university's main switchboard number, they may know what lecture he's in."

"It's…621904… oh no, sorry, 621049 I mean. Have you got the code for Exeter?"

"Yes," he replied.

"Is there anything I can do?" Rob offered.

"There's nothing anyone can do I'm afraid," he replied sadly.

Chapter 6

IT WAS A FREEZING COLD morning in early October, despite the fact the sun was shining, as Gary stood by the side of his mother's grave. His father hadn't cried. He belonged to the 'old school', and believed men shouldn't show their emotions, something that Gary had never really understood. He had cried but never in front of his father. He wept when Isabella was killed, and when he'd lost his dog, Max, at the age of fifteen, but he'd always had to do it in the privacy of his own room.

He watched the coffin being lowered into the grave, and looked over at his father. The older man's eyes were red and lined. Gary could tell by the rigidity of his father's expression that he was trying hard not to show his feelings, but the pain and grief in his eyes were beyond his powers of dissimulation.

For a moment, Gary lost his composure, "For God's sake Dad! It's Mum down there! What the hell's wrong with you," he wailed. Gary was never a demonstrative person, but he could no longer keep his agony and heartache pent up inside. He fell on his knees at the side of the grave and sobbed.

He no longer cared what people would think; he had now lost the two closest women in his life.

He expected his father to walk away, almost ashamed of his display of emotion, and was surprised when he turned to find the hand that had gently touched his shoulder was his father's, who knelt down beside his son and cried with him.

An hour or so later back at the house, Gary's Uncle Bob came over to him and gave Gary's mousey blonde hair and pale complexion an appraising glance.

"You look just like your mother, even though you don't have her black hair like Isabella," he said putting an arm around his nephew's shoulder. "I've never seen Richard show emotion like that before, even when we were children."

"Neither have I, Uncle Bob," Gary replied.

"You know, your mother was never the same since Isabella was killed," Bob continued.

"I don't think any of us were," Gary observed.

"Yes, I can appreciate that, it's just that you went away to university, so at least you had your future to look forward to, and your father threw himself into his work, doing far too many hours in my opinion. Still, I suppose that was his way of dealing with it. But your mother was at home all day with her memories. She possibly had too much time to grieve, I know her blood pressure was high and she was suffering from angina, but her doctor had kept it under control. She just gave up trying when Isabella died, and the worst of it is the bastard is out of jail and driving again!"

"How do you know?" Gary asked angrily.

"Because I saw him getting in a car outside the Plume and Feathers a few nights ago, it was obvious he'd been drinking."

"I thought he'd got three years," Gary said.

"Yeah, well I don't know, maybe he appealed, or got the sentence cut short, all I know is he's out of prison."

* * *

When Gary returned to his flat two days later he stocked up the fridge with the money his father had given him, and bought some wine.

"Shall we have Rob over and cook a meal?" he asked Jack the following day.

"I'm far too busy, I've got to complete these designs for a mock exam, I just can't be bothered," Jack replied.

It was unusual for Jack to refuse, as he was the one with culinary expertise, and could often rustle up something quite tasty from just a few scraps left in the fridge. But Gary had noticed he'd been out of sorts and irritable lately.

"It's just that what with the funeral, and everything..." Gary began.

"I know, we all feel bad about your mum, Gary, I can't tell you... okay, get Rob here around eight, and tell him to bring some booze this time, instead of drinking all of ours!"

"Will do," Gary replied, relieved that Jack had agreed, as there was something of vital importance he needed to discuss with them.

The meal was good and so was the wine. They sat in the lounge smoking when Rob got up and went over to his coat and produced a bottle of whiskey from the pocket.

"Where did you get that?" Gary asked.

"It's best you don't know," Rob replied.

"Well, let's not get ourselves into the state we did last week, I was hung over for days," Jack moaned.

They played cards, whilst they drank and smoked. Gary didn't exactly know when to broach the subject. *Perhaps they won't even remember what we were discussing. We were all so pie-eyed*, he thought.

"I don't suppose you two can remember what we were talking about the last time we were all together," Gary began.

Rob looked a little dense and confused, but Jack said quickly, "About who we'd like to exterminate, you mean," he said smiling, although his voice was deadly serious.

"Yes, I remember now," Rob began "You backed out, if my memory serves me well, said there was no one you'd want to see dead."

"Well, it was only a bit of fun wasn't it?" Gary said cautiously testing the water.

"Not to me it wasn't," Jack stated. "I would like nothing better than seeing that evil, scheming, cow dead."

"Well, I've changed my mind," Gary told them. "There *is* someone I'd like to murder!"

Jack became very excited, but he knew he

mustn't sound too enthusiastic. They would both have to think that the plan had been devised by all three of them. He reached over for the bottle and poured himself another whiskey as he lit a cigarette.

He said complacently, "It could be done quite easily." Gary and Rob looked confused. "But before I elaborate, I want to know just who it is you'd like to see dead. Surely, you haven't suddenly gained a vicious enemy, in such a short space of time." He had to make sure that Gary's intentions were serious.

He told them about Tony Mulligan, the man who had killed his sister and been imprisoned for drunken driving. He told them that, in his opinion, Mulligan was also responsible for his mother's death.

"Well, you don't really know that," Rob said.

Jack was annoyed with Rob, there was no way he wanted Gary to change his mind, but he needn't have been concerned, as Gary was adamant when he answered Rob. "That drunken bastard took Isabella's life, she had the world at her feet... a talented dancer... and then..."

His eyes started to fill with tears, but the anger superseded his emotions "We all missed her, but I had uni, dad has his career, but mum just moped about the house all day grieving. Bob, Dad's brother, reckoned it finally finished Mom off."

Jack was just about to agree that the man was responsible for both deaths when Gary continued. "And would you believe, the bastard's out of prison and driving again. Most likely drunk, I wonder what poor sod he'll kill next and wreck their family!"

"None, if we get to him first," Jack announced, "Now pour yourself another drink. If you listen to me we can dispose of all three of them."

"You're talking rubbish! You'd never get away with it. If Miranda died you'd be the first person the police would turn to," Gary told Jack, "I mean, you've threatened her in public, everyone knows you hate her guts. And if Tony Mulligan was suddenly found murdered, my family would be the first people the police would suspect, since he'd killed Isabella."

"I see what you mean, I had that fight with Paul Ramsey, if you remember," Rob began "Still it was worth it to see him with a black eye and a broken arm, after what he'd done to Claire."

"Well, 'an eye for an eye and a tooth for a

tooth,' according to the old saying. Still a black eye for a life, not much in the way of retribution," Jack commented.

"Okay, I see your point, but again if anything happened to Ramsey, in fact if anyone even hurt a single hair on his head, I'd be the first one they'd come looking for, it's hopeless, I tell you."

"I take it neither of you have seen the Alfred Hitchcock film, *Strangers on a Train*?" Jack remarked.

There was silence for a few moments and then Gary said, "Dad's got all his films on video. I remember now, two men plan to kill each other's wives while the other one has an alibi."

"Precisely," Jack said.

Rob and Gary both looked a little at sea, so Jack began to explain.

"For the sake of simplicity, let's say we all want, A, B, and C dead. Each of us has a motive of sorts. So I suggest I get rid of A for you Gary, you get rid of B for me and so on… At the time of each death, we all make sure we have alibis, in fact perfect alibis. So there's no way any of us can even figure as a suspect, once they've been checked out."

"I can't believe what I'm hearing," Rob said amazed.

"Why not? It all makes sense," Jack replied.

"I know it makes sense, but you're talking like we're doing a rota for household chores, not planning three murders."

"The best laid plans are the simplest. Just as an example, let's say you Gary, could get rid of Miranda for me. If I knew the deed would be committed say between six and midnight on a particular day. I could say, go out with friends for a meal, and make sure I was with them at all times. I could even arrange to be miles away, making it impossible for me to have been anywhere in the vicinity of the murder, let alone involved. As I said, the 'Perfect Alibi'."

"Okay, I know you hate her, and you have good cause, but she's done nothing to me, I couldn't kill her," Gary stated.

"Well, that evil, drunken bastard who killed your sister and mother has personally done nothing to me, but that wouldn't stop me killing him for you, or perhaps you'd prefer to wait until he smashes some other poor sod up in his car," Jack replied.

"No, I want him dead, but I'd rather kill him myself."

"Oh you would, would you? Get banged up in prison, the end of your career, and what about your dad, you're all he's got left now. Do you want him to spend the rest of his life visiting you in some hell hole?"

Gary's mind was in turmoil. "I know what you're saying makes sense Jack, it's just that the only thing is…"

"Come on, spit it out," Jack told him, "We're either all in this one hundred percent or we're out. I don't want any doubts or misgivings. If either of you are even slightly apprehensive or unsure it can't work out."

"Okay, that Mulligan bloke has killed Gary's sister," Rob began, "and contributed to his mother's death, so in my opinion he's a murderer. Paul Ramsey was definitely responsible for Claire's death. She would never have taken that overdose, but for him. Whereas with Miranda, okay, she's a bitch and no one likes her, she rips off people's ideas and passes them off as her own, but she's never actually done anyone any harm, I mean, does she deserve to die?"

"I worked day and night on my last collection," Jack began to explain, "I put my heart and soul into it, it was my baby, and she passed it off as her own, and there are other things, which I don't want to discuss. I believe wholeheartedly that you both have been desperately wronged, and yet you don't have faith in me. It will never work out, I suppose we ought to forget the whole thing. We have to trust each other completely, if there's even the slightest doubt, it's useless."

"What are these other things that Miranda's done?" Gary asked remembering how she'd enticed him into bed just to get hold of Jack's designs.

"I can't really tell you in detail. It's just that she did the dirty on someone else, wrecked their life in fact, but that's all I'm prepared to say..."

"Well, that's good enough for me," Rob announced, looking at Gary. "What about you?"

He nodded in agreement. "Okay," he replied.

Jack inwardly sighed with relief.

Bloody hell. That was a close one. Still, I think I've convinced them, and luckily they haven't bombarded me with questions.

"The only thing is..." Gary began.

Oh no, here it comes Jack thought.

"I don't know if I could kill anyone, as I've always hated violence," Gary confessed.

"Yeah, I remember now, that rumpus in the student bar," Rob said grinning. "That kid punched me in the face and I had a nose bleed, and yet you were the one who felt faint… Perhaps we ought to forget the whole thing, you are bloody useless."

Gary stood up. "Now look here Rob…"

"Hang on, you were the one who mentioned it first," Rob said as he downed the remains of his whiskey.

"There are lots of ways of disposing of someone, without violence or even spilling a drop of blood, that's no problem, but you two are." Jack said.

"What do you mean?" they asked in unison.

"Well, for a start, Rob, taking the piss about Gary, and then you taking offence. We have got to support one another to the hilt. This is a confidence pact between us, if we carry it through it must never go any further than these four walls. We have to swear to one another that this secret will remain between the three of us until our death," Jack explained.

"Yes, well that goes without saying, surely," Rob added.

"Does it? I mean never divulge it to a girlfriend or even a wife in years to come, no matter how close we may be to them."

"Well it's not exactly the sort of thing you

could mention. She would probably end up leaving you, that's if she didn't go to the police first," Gary remarked.

"So what if one of us gets drunk or high on drugs, and we accidentally let something out?" Rob suggested. "What happens then?"

"If that was ever to happen, you'd just have to say it was all a farce, and just the drink talking. If you were in a state, no one would probably believe you anyway. I mean it would be so far fetched and incredible. In fact I can hardly believe we're discussing doing away with three people," Gary replied.

Jack knew that Rob and Gary would have to be completely convinced and committed, as once his plan was in motion, there could be no turning back or second thoughts which could be dangerous for all of them, if there was a weak link in the chain.

"Listen," Jack began, "I know you've both said you're committed, but I want you to sleep on it for the next couple of days. I don't want either of you going into this unless you're absolutely certain. If anyone chickens out at the last minute, it could be disastrous for the other two. But if we are all committed and careful, and carry out instructions to the letter, then there'll be no problems."

Rob left the flat feeling a little depressed. It was a bit of an anti climax, as he was raring to go ahead with the plan, and had no qualms whatsoever. When he aired his doubts, it was only to see the reaction of the other two. He had always felt he'd never really achieved anything his life, although he was only 22. Unlike Jack and Gary, he wasn't clever and he just worked full time in the local pub. One could probably understand a middle aged person looking back at their life with certain regrets at perhaps not achieving certain goals, but not someone as young as Rob. His insecure family background probably hadn't helped. His parents were divorced when he was barely a teenager, and he stayed with his mother for a year or two, but never really hit it off with the new man in her life, so he ended up living with his dad but they fought like cat and dog. His sister, who was ten years older than Rob, was living with her boyfriend when their parents spilt up, so it never really affected her in the way it did Rob, and now she was married with a young family, and seemed to be settled and content.

His thoughts went back to Claire. She had been the only person he had really cared for. The fact that she was on drugs wasn't a major problem for him, as he was confident that with his love and support, she could kick the habit. He had felt it a personal challenge, and that he now had a goal in life, if he could get her to give up, at least he would have done some good. The struggle was difficult for both of them, trying to overcome her addiction to cocaine. He began to think about what had happened... *She would have beaten it wouldn't she?* he asked himself.

For God's sake, you know she would. It was all his fault, he more or less murdered her. He might just as well have pushed the needle in himself, or is Ramsey just the cop-out, because she'd gone back on the drugs.

Rob suddenly had a slight doubt, even though he told everyone in his opinion Ramsey has been responsible for her death, but to admit Ramsey was entirely to blame for Claire's death, was almost like admitting he had failed in getting her to break the habit.

Surely if she had loved him, she wouldn't have done it, although the doctor said she was so unstable it only needed one small thing to make her crack. For God's sake! What's wrong with you, man? You're planning this bloke's murder, you can't have any bloody doubts, he told himself. *Yeah well, he bloody killed her and he's going to pay.*

He was determined he wouldn't let any doubt creep back into his mind. To him, to get revenge was the only thing he could do for Claire now.

Chapter 7

"DO YOU KNOW, I feel like I've personally let them down."

"Who?" Andrew said as he looked up from his newspaper.

"Sophie Bryan's parents. They need justice and I haven't been able to get it for them. I feel that in all my years in the force, I've never had a case I couldn't solve sooner or later. I mean there were always those that seemed hopeless at times, and I did think I might never crack it, but eventually something would always turn up or I'd manage to work it out."

"You know how it is, Andrew, you get some information that would seem of no consequence and trivial at some stage in the investigation, but then it would suddenly become relevant, and things that had puzzled and bewildered us for so long would suddenly become clear."

"Well, in this case there is no motive," he replied, looking at her tired and drawn face.

He walked over to where she was sitting on the lounge chair, and started to massage her shoulders.

"You've examined every possible angle. What more could you have done?" he asked.

"Oh, I don't know. I must have missed something."

"You know, Jo, it really annoys me when you take all the responsibility for these cases on your own shoulders. If you missed something, then so did Bill, the Chief, forensics and the rest of the team." He stopped massaging her and said, "Want a drink to relax you? My therapeutic touch doesn't seem to be working as well as it usually does. You still seem tense."

"Yes, that would be nice," she replied.

A few minutes later Andrew returned with a bottle of Chardonnay and two glasses.

"Do you want to carry on talking about it?" he asked.

"Not if it's annoying you," Josephine replied sarcastically. "Okay I'm sorry," she said, looking at the hurt in his face.

"Let's go through it again, although I've lost count of the times Bill and I have trodden this path to the point where he was so frustrated and bored he ended up at the pub."

"I never thought I'd say this about Bill, but I sympathise with him," Andrew said teasingly. "I know we've been through this before when I did a profile for you in my professional capacity as a forensic psychologist, but the only other alternative is that it was a serial killer. As there have been no similar murders since, it can only be, as we speculated, some crazed lunatic who had to kill at the time of the eclipse. The murderer might not even be local—many people travelled from the other end of the country to Devon just for the eclipse, and if he's one of them you're looking for a needle in a haystack."

"Whether it's a crazed lunatic or a serial killer, it's no consolation to her parents. Maybe we're using that theory as a cop out because we haven't a clue as to who did it," Josephine remarked.

"So let's be logical," Andrew began, "what can you do? You've exhausted every possible line of enquiry. If there was any one area you hadn't explored, then I'd say look into it. I'm afraid, Josephine, that on this occasion you haven't been able to catch the culprit. You are not superhuman or infallible, and you've got to accept that this may be a case you can never solve."

"I'm a failure," she announced lethargically.

"Don't be so bloody stupid. I know it sounds callous, but you can't win them all," he said angrily.

"Well try explaining that to Sophie Bryan's parents. Can't you imagine what they are going through?"

"Of course I can, I'm not that hard and uncaring, if you think that then I don't know why the hell you are with me," he snapped.

"Of course I don't... I'm sorry," she uttered.

"Look Josephine, even if you found her murderer, it can't bring their daughter back, so it may be of little consolation."

"Yes I can see your point to a certain extent, but if it was Jessica I couldn't rest until I knew who it was, and that I had them under lock and key," she told him.

"That's because it's your profession," he explained. "Maybe all they want now is for their daughter to rest in peace, and just have fond memories of her. Can't you just leave it at that?"

"I wish I could, Andrew, I really do. It's just eating away at me."

"Well there's nothing else I can say, so I won't even try."

Andrew intended to broach the subject of marriage again and ask if Josephine had come to a decision, but he knew the time was far from right, so decided to leave it on hold for the time being.

Jack Stanford had mapped out his intricate plan to murder some time beforehand. He had already devised what he thought to be a foolproof strategy of events, methods and plots to take the lives of three people, although at the time he was concocting his plan, he didn't know precisely who the other two victims would be. Now he did, he would be able to monitor their movements. He knew he couldn't risk producing his proposals too soon, as the others might wonder how he had managed to contrive such an intricate plan in a relatively short time. He couldn't risk them becoming even slightly suspicious, so he waited a week or so, before he arranged to go through the details. He'd already made one fatal mistake and couldn't risk another one.

Jack knew he could take a life by any one of a number of ways. He wasn't at all squeamish, although he didn't like methods that involved much blood loss, because of the risk involved. Having read up on forensic pathology he realised that, due to the advances in technology, a killer could be caught by something as simple as a stray hair or a minute spot of blood. In his plan the original prime suspects would be eliminated, and the chances of suspicion falling on the murderer was minimal, if not beyond the bounds of possibility. Even though the potential suspects would be a healthy distance away at the time of the murder with steadfast alibis, there was always a chance the assailant could be spotted. This would have to be reduced to a minimum: he just couldn't take the chance that the other two might be caught. If one of them weakened the entire plan could be divulged to the police.

He knew the only person he could rely on one hundred percent was himself.

Okay so Rob and Gary were his friends and under any other circumstances they would be loyal, but faced with a murder charge, it would be human nature to say anything to save themselves. The murders would have to be quick, clean and quiet if possible. And if all went smoothly... Still, even the best laid plans...

A week later, they had a meeting to discuss a plan that would change their lives forever.

But the first thing that would have to happen would be that Gary needed to leave the flat they shared. If they were still living together, it might cause the police to put two and two together.

He knew Gary wouldn't be pleased with the arrangement, but it was something he would have to do. Jack had already got a bedsit lined up for him, and the rent was reasonable.

Since Gary had slept with Miranda, even though she had only succumbed in order to get her hands on Jack's designs and Gary now had no feelings for her, other than those of regret about what had occurred, he felt he could not end her life. So it was agreed that he should dispose of the tutor Paul Ramsey, who was Rob's enemy.

Jack would kill Tony Mulligan and take pleasure in doing so, not just because of his sadistic trait, but because he felt he was doing the public a favour, as this man would never drink or drive again, so other lives might be saved.

Jack knew down to the finest detail how he would dispose of his victim, but first he had to make certain that Gary and Rob would carry out their instructions to the letter. Before he gave them their plans of action he needed to check out the layout of the building where Paul Ramsey worked. His plan of action for his victim, Tony Mulligan, and Gary's victim, Paul Ramsey, would be as quick and clean as possible. He was tempted to make Miranda's death painful and torturous, as he hated her so much, but since Rob was carrying out this dastardly deed for him, he knew that it would not be possible.

They decided to meet in a pub several miles away from the one they usually frequented, the Duck and Drake where Rob worked, as although people probably knew they were acquainted, they didn't want to be seen sitting in a corner huddled together, discussing their plan.

"So, how far apart are these things going to take place?" Gary asked, he was loath to use the word 'murders'.

"I don't know yet," Jack began, "at this moment, all I'm really concerned about is that everything goes off smoothly. Now how come you didn't tell me Ramsey was a diabetic?" he asked Rob.

"Because I didn't know," he replied.

"Well I've found out that he is, and also that he uses the fourth floor lecture room lab every Thursday morning, in the new wing, that at the moment is hardly ever used. He takes group six for chemistry. It overlooks a field at the rear, and hardly anyone ever goes there, there are just trees and bushes below. Due to lack of funds, the gardeners have just left it as almost a wilderness."

"I wouldn't bank on the fact no one ever goes there," Gary corrected him, "it's an ideal place for students to go for sex or to take drugs."

"Well that's normally at night. I suppose there's a remote chance someone might be there in the morning, but I doubt it," Jack replied.

"Well if you're planning for me to bump him off there, do you mind telling me how I get him to go to that spot?" Gary asked.

"You don't... now just let me explain... I just need to make sure if he opens a window and calls for help, no one will see or hear him. If you follow my instructions carefully, yours will be the easiest crime of them all. No blood, no screams, in fact you don't even have to be there at the time of his death."

Gary looked relieved, if not exactly pleased.

"Now listen carefully, this is what you have to do..." Jack began.

Chapter 8

PAUL RAMSEY sat in the staff room and opened up his battered old brown leather briefcase. He started to sort out his papers for the lecture he had to take in the new wing.

The fourth floor of the building was a bit off the beaten track. When the extension had been built, it housed sixteen rooms, three of which were due to be equipped as science laboratories, but because of lack of funds, there was only enough money left to equip one. All the other rooms were empty. Some tutors found it a bit dismal and quiet, but it didn't bother Ramsey. He liked the fact that he didn't have noisy students walking up and down the corridor outside, while he was taking the lecture.

He looked the typical 'old professor' type, in his old brown tweed jacket with leather inserts at the elbows, which he wore with a white shirt and paisley tie. He tried, unsuccessfully, to tame his thinning, yet somewhat unruly, dark hair with Brylcreem.

Some thought Ramsey the old fashioned type of teacher, who was dedicated to his profession and cared more for the students' success than his pay cheque at the end of the month. Those who did have that impression about the man were completely wrong. His attitude was, if the students didn't put in the necessary effort and dedication to get the results they needed, then that was their hard luck.

He was loath to spend any extra time helping students revise, or giving them extra tuition. Even the dedicated ones who really wanted to succeed got no praise or encouragement, even when they had worked well.

The ones who knew the 'real Ramsey' were amazed at how he'd managed to hold on to his position at the university for as long as he had. It was probably that the required amount of students had got the grades in their degrees, even though it was because of their own efforts, not his teaching skills.

He knew his subject, he just couldn't relate to his students, rather like a doctor with no bedside manner...only worse.

Five minutes or so later, Fiona Roberts, who was the French tutor, entered the staff room and poured herself a coffee from the Cona machine.

"Would you like one, Paul?" she asked.

"Yes, okay. It might keep me awake while I'm talking to those morons," he answered grimly.

Just at that moment another member of staff, Jake Turner, entered the room.

"What's happened to your car?" he asked Ramsey.

"What do you mean?"

"All the side window's shattered. It looks like someone's thrown a rock or something through it," he replied.

Paul Ramsey hurried out of the staff room looking rather flustered.

"I've got to see this!" Fiona giggled like an excited child.

"Me too, miserable old sod," Jake agreed, and they followed him out to the staff car park.

"Bastards!" Ramsey shouted, when he reached his car.

"It's a pity it's not your windscreen, as that would have been covered by your car insurance. Still, you can phone the services. Who are you with? The AA or the RAC?"

"Neither," Ramsey replied, "they're just a rip-off. I'll have to take it to a small garage I know. The chap who runs it is quite reasonable, he's done jobs on the car before."

"I wouldn't leave it too long; rain's forecast for this afternoon," Fiona told him.

When they returned to the staff room, Ramsey began, "I'd cancel the bloody lecture if I could, but I haven't turned up to this group before, and they've got an exam at the end of the month, worse luck!"

"You go ahead with the lecture, and I'll put some thick plastic I've got over the window. You can take it to the garage afterwards," Jake offered.

"Oh… well… thanks… if you don't mind…" Ramsey said, rather surprised. It wasn't just the students who disliked him, but most of the staff as well. So it wasn't often someone offered to do him a favour, but Jake was doing it as much for the students as for Ramsey.

He quickly put his notes back into the briefcase, and made his way to the lecture.

"Miserable old sod! Serves him right!" Fiona said, picking up her cup of cold coffee.

When he reached the science lab on the fourth floor, his students were already seated, waiting for him. He put his briefcase on the table and said, "Now, we've got a lot to get through this morning. It's a two-hour lecture, and it's past ten o'clock now. I need to be away before twelve o'clock as I've got an appointment, so I'll have to rush."

"What's new?" one student said to another.

For some reason, Ramsey was more helpful to the students than usual. He answered their questions, and assisted them in the experiments. Whether this change in attitude was because he needed to get away quickly or the fact that he was pleased at Jake's offer to cover the window for him was a mystery.

By eleven fifty the lecture was over, and the lab equipment packed away neatly. As the students were leaving, he said, "Good luck with your exam next week," before going back inside to put his paperwork away.

He never heard the door being locked from outside, as he mooched through his briefcase.

I'll probably be a couple of hours or so at the garage, so I'll do my insulin injection now, he thought, glancing at his watch... *that's funny, I could have sworn... oh, perhaps I left it in the staff room.*

He closed his briefcase and hurried to the door. As he went to open it, it wouldn't budge.

"What the hell?" he said out loud, as he turned the handle for a few seconds. "The damn thing's stuck."

111

After a minute or so had passed, he realised the door was locked.

Bloody stupid caretaker! What does he think he's playing at? I'll have to ring him on my mobile.

He went back to the table, opened his briefcase again and searched through it.

What? No mobile? Surely I didn't leave that in the staff room; I can't even remember getting it out.

He sat at the desk for a minute or so, not alarmed or frightened; just angry as he began to think someone was playing a trick on him.

It was only when it reached one o'clock that he started to get anxious, as his insulin was now due. He began to feel a little weak and sweaty. He'd usually carry a chocolate biscuit or a banana with him, for emergencies, but hadn't bothered on this particular day.

He sat down, trying to figure out what he should do. It would be no good banging on the door, as no one would hear him since the new wing was deserted. There was no phone in the lab, and the fire alarm was outside in the corridor. Each option he thought of was useless. His heart pumped faster as his vision began to blur…

The window… yes, that's it…I can call for help…

He got up and staggered over, but the catch was stuck, and by now he was so weak he couldn't budge it.

My God…what can I do?

Suddenly he noticed a metal tripod on a nearby bench. He picked it up and with what strength he had left, he flung it at the window. As it went crashing through the glass shattered over him and the floor. The tripod landed in the dense undergrowth below, making hardly a sound.

Ramsey hung his head out of the window and gave a weak cry for help. Even if he had screamed at the top of his voice, it was doubtful he would have been heard, due to the position of the building. The broken glass cut his hands as his bloodstained fingers grabbed hold of the metal ledge, and he slid down the wall, making a long bloody smear with his fingers.

"Please… help…" he murmured weakly, as he fell on the floor and into a diabetic coma.

He lay there peacefully for a further two hours before he died.

Chapter 9

DC SALLY JAMES entered Josephine's office. "I've just received a call from DS Charlie Morgan, ma'am" she began. "There's been a death at Exeter University, they thought it might have just been an accident, only he feels one or two things indicate foul play, he's at the scene now if you can get over there."

"No problem. Is Bill about anywhere?"

"He's gone to the dentist," Sally replied.

"What! I wouldn't have thought wild horses could have dragged him there, he's such a coward," Josephine remarked.

"He reckons he's only having a scrape and polish."

"That what he thinks, the dentist will have a field day when he looks in Bill's mouth, he'll probably be drilling all day," Josephine joked as she reached for her bag.

"Ring DS Morgan back and tell him we're on our way, and leave a message for Bill to join us when he gets back."

As the police car pulled up in the car park, Josephine recalled coming to this same place some weeks earlier, when she had spoken to the staff about Sophie Bryan, although she placed no importance or connection to that fact.

As a PC and a member of staff took her to the new wing, she noticed how empty and desolate the building appeared, despite the police presence. It was as if the tutor could read her mind when he said, "There wasn't any money left when this wing was built, so all the other lecture rooms and laboratories have remained empty."

"Sounds like the wards in the NHS hospitals," Josephine remarked.

When she arrived at the murder scene DS Charlie Morgan came up to her.

"DI Blake, I haven't seen you in ages, how are things ma'am?"

"Fine and yourself, family all okay?"

"Well, they are teenagers now, you know," he replied.

"I'd like to say Jessica had passed that stage, but I'm not so sure, possibly in years, but not in the way of problems. Anyway, down to work, fill me in," Josephine told him.

"Right, the victim's name is Paul Ramsey, and he's a Science lecturer, the doctor believes he died of a diabetic coma, due to lack of insulin," Morgan informed her.

"So what have we to indicate foul play?" She asked.

"The door was locked from the outside, as there's no sign of a key in the lab, and no way he could get out. He had no insulin on him, and the fact that the window has been smashed, points to the fact he was trying to attract someone's attention for help."

"No phones in here then?" Josephine said looking around.

"No, and he didn't have his mobile on him, which one member of staff, a Mr Jake Turner said he usually carried with him at all times. He gave a chemistry lesson in this room, that ended just before midday, the students left about that time, leaving Ramsey alone in the lab."

As she walked over to where the huddled body she asked the police doctor, "Any idea about time of death?"

"I'd say he probably died about four hours ago or thereabouts, but he would have lost consciousness quite some time before that. I can't tell you much more, that's down to the forensic pathologist, but the cuts on his fingers are from the broken glass, and there are no signs of violence on the body. So it could be a natural death, well if you could call it that".

Several pictures of the body were taken from different angles as the SOCO team examined the room. "Since they had about twenty students doing experiments, at the lecture, he may have got up close to several of them, so it's possible he may have particles from their clothing on his body, which could prove difficult," DS Morgan told Josephine.

"I'll need to speak to the students that attended the class, and also the deceased's colleagues."

"We can arrange to speak to the University's Dean, Dr Etherington, he can get the students and staff assembled and available for questioning," Morgan informed her.

Just at that moment Brian Morrison arrived.

"I'll leave you to it then," Josephine told him, "and ring you tomorrow, there's not a lot we can do now, arrange for the door to be locked when Dr Morrison's finished, and we'll have to leave a PC on duty. I also want the entire building sealed off, not just this room," she told Morgan. Just as she was about to leave Bill came to the door looking ghastly and holding his mouth.

"Don't tell me," Josephine began before Bill had a chance to speak. "You've had to have a filling."

"Three," he said in a mumbled voice, hardly

able to speak with the numbness of the injection. "Anything I can do?"

"No, I'll give you all the details on the way back in the car."

* * *

"I've never known Paul Ramsey to be without his insulin pen or mobile phone," the Dean, Dr Etherington, told Josephine as she sat in his office.

"When we searched his house, we found a stock of insulin and needles still in their packaging, but there was no trace of the pen he'd been using or his mobile phone. So he didn't forget them on that particular day, and leave them at home."

"I've asked the caretaker, Joe Evans, to come and see you, as he is responsible for locking all the lecture rooms at the end of the day," Dr Etherington told her.

A few minutes or so later he arrived at the office. "Inspector Blake here, would like a few words with you," the Dean told him.

"Certainly sir, whatever the lady would like to know," Joe Evans replied.

"Do you want me to leave?" Dr Etherington asked.

"No, please stay. Now Mr Evans," Josephine began. "I take it you are responsible for locking the rooms."

"Yes, that's correct. There may be the odd occasion where a tutor or student needs to stay behind very late for some reason, and they may ask for a key, but it's usually my responsibility."

"So yesterday, was anyone else due to use that room?"

"No, after Mr Ramsey's chemistry class, it would not have been used again for the rest of the day," he told her.

"So would he have locked the door when he left?"

"No, I'd go in to the new wing at about five o'clock if I knew the room would be used just to check the building and lock the room. In the new wing, although there are several rooms, this one was the only equipped laboratory in use."

"Surely, to leave it open until the early evening, with expensive equipment in there would be an ideal opportunity for a thief or vandal," Josephine observed.

"Usually the room would be used both morning and afternoon, and I'd go up and lock it at about five, when the last lecture was over."

"Do you have the keys for the other rooms in that wing?" she asked.

"Yes, but they were never used," he replied.

"So for someone to come along and lock the door from the outside, which is what we believed happened, so that Mr Ramsey couldn't get out, would they have to come to your office to get a key?"

"Well… yes… I suppose, I have the keys hanging on individual hooks with the block and room number above them."

"So, in this case, the key would be on a hook which said above New Wing Room forty-four, and did you notice if that key was missing at all, during the day?" Josephine asked.

"Well I don't think it was, but I couldn't be sure. It was on the hook at four o'clock when I collected the keys to begin my rounds of inspection."

"But surely you have a duplicate set in case one gets lost or mislaid," the Dean suggested.

"Yes, that's right sir, they are locked away in the safe."

"So can we assume," Josephine suggested, "it's possible someone came into your office when you weren't there, removed the key, locked Mr Ramsey in the room, and then returned it later to it's original place."

"I suppose it's possible, but yesterday, I was there most of the time. I can remember Miss Moran, asking for the key to the gym, as she was stopping till later in the evening, but there was no one else," Joe Evans replied.

"It's feasible that the key could have been taken at an earlier date, and a duplicate made," she suggested.

"Mmm... Well... yes that could have occurred, but I do try to be security conscious, you know that, don't you sir?" He looked at the Dean rather worried and apprehensively.

"No one is blaming you Joe. Look Inspector, we've never had any cause to complain, as far as I'm concerned our caretaker does a good job".

"I'm not inferring that he's not trustworthy or reliable, but I'm simply trying to establish how someone could have got hold of a key," Josephine stated.

"Now, going back, when you went to room forty-four and found it already locked, did you find it strange?"

"Not at first, as I've said there are odd times when tutors will lock the doors."

"So why did you open the door to the lab and go in?"

"I still needed to check that all the windows were shut, and switches turned off, just a general safety check. That's when I noticed the smashed glass in the window, and when I went over, there was Mr Ramsey lying on the ground. So I contacted the police," he explained.

"Well you did all anyone could under the circumstances," Josephine assured him.

"If you do think of anything else that might help, someone suspicious hanging about, or how anyone could get hold of the keys, please ring me," she said as she handed Joe Evans a card.

"Will that be all sir, only I've got a lot to do?" he said looking at the Dean.

"Yes you get on, thank you Joe," he replied.

After he had left, Josephine asked Dr Etherington, "What can you tell me about Paul Ramsey?"

"I've known him for the last five years," he began. "He wasn't the easiest person to get on with, a bit of the 'old school type', and unfortunately that didn't go down too well with the students or fellow members of staff. I know this sounds contradictory, he was a clever man, but not a very good teacher. I've had him before me once or twice, when people have made complaints."

" What was his reaction to that?" Josephine inquired.

"Oh he'd improve for a week or two, and then go back to his old ways. You know to begin with, he was very anti mobile phones, as he wasn't keen on many modern-day devices, he always said he wouldn't be able to get away from people with one of those things. He did get one, and just turned it off when he didn't want to be disturbed. But in the finish, he found his mobile a godsend, and just like his insulin, he would carry it with him at all times. I suppose if he'd had them on him... he'd still be alive now."

"Well, that's my opinion. The door was locked from the outside, and I think it was done purposely, in fact his mobile could have been stolen along with the insulin, as they have never been found, either in the staff room, or at his home. I've got PCs searching the grounds, but I'd guess that whoever took them has probably disposed of them miles away," Josephine told him.

"So you believe someone took them purposely?"

"Most definitely, there was foul play. He was locked in the room and his two life-saving forms of communication and survival removed, so he couldn't summon help. It was unfortunate for Ramsey that the room was in such a quiet spot. In fact perhaps the murderer arranged it that way, as it would be unlikely that anyone would hear his cries for help," she suggested.

"I thought it was just a terrible accident..." the Dean observed.

"I believe, Dr Etherington, that Paul Ramsey's death was due to a rather clever and well-instigated plan."

Josephine was in the incident room with Bill and the rest of the team, she had just finished going through the facts of the case with them all.

Bill stood up. "After talking to several students, and members of staff at the university, I can tell you, categorically, the man was not popular."

"So are we looking for anyone specific, Sarge?" one DC asked.

"No, but I'd say there are several possibilities, I couldn't find anyone who had a decent thing to say about the man."

"It's odd that say, at least one of the students, didn't leave with him, if he hadn't been in the room totally alone, perhaps the murderer wouldn't have locked the door," DC Sally James suggested.

"I don't think he was the sort of person that the students felt that they could stay behind with to ask anything, and they said he was in a rush to leave, something about his car," Bill replied.

"Yes, apparently his car window had been smashed earlier that morning," Josephine began. "It's possible it was done deliberately, so that his assailant could remove his phone and insulin, while he was checking the damage."

"The window hasn't been repaired yet, so we can always get forensics to check the car over, something might show up," Bill suggested.

"Mmm, that would be worth looking into, I'll get on to them," Josephine replied.

She went on to explain about her findings after talking with the caretaker. She suggested that if someone hadn't removed the key to room forty-four, on the day of Ramsey's death, they could have done so beforehand, and got a duplicate made.

"That's a good point, quite possible," Bill agreed, "but if that was the case, it suggests the killer had been planning this sometime beforehand."

"Most definitely, they must have known quite a lot about Ramsey; his movements, times of his lectures, the fact he was diabetic. Most importantly they must have known about the location of the room, and the fact it would be difficult, if not impossible for him to draw attention to himself, or make himself heard," Josephine added.

"Surely then, that points to the murder being a student or member of staff, if they had that particular knowledge," one DS suggested.

"It does appear that way, I agree," Josephine remarked, "but then again I suppose anyone could find out his agenda, just by looking at his time tables and seminar groups."

"Some might say the location was a definite advantage to the killer. The room being on the fourth floor, and overlooking virtually nothing except shrubs and trees," Bill added.

"So let's assure it's someone at the university for the time being, we now need to look for motive. What do we know about his private life?"

"Not a lot at present ma'am," one DC said looking at his notes. "He was single, lived alone, no children. We've contacted a brother who lives in Oxford, but it seems they weren't close; used to send each other a card at Christmas and birthdays, and that's about it. His brother described Ramsey as a very private person, but he couldn't tell us if he had any enemies," he concluded.

"We need to speak to his colleagues again, obviously someone needed to get rid of him for some reason. There could be any amount of reasons, but until we know more about him, we are just clutching at straws," Josephine remarked.

"Nothing's come up from forensics as yet," Bill told Josephine and the team. "Since he actually died in a locked room, with no signs of violence, except the cuts on his hands, which were self-inflicted, when he threw the apparatus out of the window in a last vain attempt to attract attention. It doesn't look optimistic, although Brian Morrison is still examining the body in the hope that something, however minor, might come to light."

"Right, let's get down to work," Josephine began turning to DC Sally James, "I want you to interview the students that were at the lecture again, those were the last people to see him before his death. You know the sort of thing, did he appear tense? Anything strange about his manner? Bill, could you talk to the members of staff again, and I'll go back and see the Dean."

"I thought you'd already spoken to him," Bill remarked.

"I did, but he must know more. I mean it's his responsibility to know about his staff."

"But people don't talk about their private lives," Bill added.

"I know there may be a part to Ramsey's character that's completely alien to Dr Etherington, but I just feel he must know more about the man, than he's letting on. Oh and DC Barnes."

"Yes ma'am?"

"Speak to Ramsey's doctor again. Find out how long he's been diabetic, how serious his condition was, and how long he'd been on his present type of medication etc."

"I'll get on to that right away," Barnes told her.

"Well, you're a better man than me, if you can get an appointment to see him. You can never get to see a doctor at my practice, day or night, even if you're dying."

"Don't exaggerate Bill," Josephine uttered.

"I'm not! The receptionist on duty guards the doctors, like the crown jewels. You stand more chance of winning the lottery. I mean if you phone on Monday…"

"Right, then," Josephine said loudly, interrupting Bill's moaning. "Let's get on, unless anyone has any other questions." No one in the team answered so they ended the briefing.

Chapter 10

THREE DAYS LATER DC Sally James was in Josephine's office. "It seems, there's a bit of a question mark over the death of a former student of Ramsey's. A Claire Savage," she began.

"Apparently she was on drugs, but with the help of her boyfriend she was kicking the habit. Ramsey marked some paper rather badly, and she went to see him. He told her she was useless and would never make it as a scientist, or words to that effect. In fact he more or less told her to give up the degree course. She took an overdose a few days later. Understandably her boyfriend was devastated, blamed Ramsey totally, and said he caused Claire to commit suicide, although the coroner's report was accidental death. No one really knew if she intended to kill herself, but everyone I spoke to seemed to think that Ramsey was the reason she went back on the drugs. One of the students told me Claire's boyfriend, Rob Morton, went to one of his lectures and threatened him, and then proceeded to beat the hell out of him. A student, Mike Sears, apparently had to pull him off with the help of one or two others."

"That sounds promising Sally, well done. I think I'll arrange to see this Mike Sears, when I visit the Dean, and find out more about the incident."

Unfortunately Josephine had something else that needed attending to on the day of her meeting with Dr Etherington, so Bill took her place. He would have preferred to speak to Mike Sears alone, so he asked the Dean if he would mind leaving them alone during the interview. He looked a little put out at Bill's request but said, "That's no problem, I need to see one of the tutors anyway, I'll be back shortly." Sears looked relieved that the Dean had left them alone.

"Look, I know Rob Morton is your friend, but I really need to find out exactly what went on," Bill began.

"I wouldn't be dropping him in it, so to speak, as the attack was common knowledge all over the campus, even though Rob isn't a student here."

"I wasn't aware of that?" Bill confessed.

"He works at the pub, where all the students drink, so we all know him. As you know Rob attacked Ramsey in front of loads of people".

"What happened exactly?" Bill enquired.

"Rob had threatened him before, apparently, burst into one of his lectures and called him a murdering bastard. Rob said he might as well have killed Claire with his bare hands. Ramsey phoned security, and had him removed, but Rob must have got back in without them knowing, because he was waiting for him in the corridor afterwards. He laid into him good and proper, Ramsey had a black eye, and a broken arm, as well as a few cracked ribs."

"Did anyone attempt to help Ramsey?" Bill asked.

"Not to start with, they all despised him and said afterwards he got what he deserved".

"I was led to believe two of them helped you drag Rob off him during the assault?"

"That was because we were worried that if Rob did any more damage, he might end up killing Ramsey. So we separated them, but more for Rob's sake really, I didn't want him on some assault, or worse still, murder charge." Sears explained.

"We don't have any record of charges being made against him," Bill disclosed.

"No… Well… It seems Ramsey wouldn't press charges, which surprised everyone. Maybe deep down he knew he was partly responsible for Claire's death."

"Surely the Dean, Dr Etherington, would have insisted," Bill remarked.

"To be honest, I don't think he wanted any more bad publicity for the University, as Claire's death was in the paper, and there were reporters milling round the campus for a day or two," Sears replied.

"Right, I think that's all, thank you for your co-operation, I'll have to speak to Rob Morton," Bill concluded.

"I feel awful for him, I'd never drop a mate in it, still everyone knew about the assault," Mike said before leaving.

* * *

Fifteen minutes or so later the Dean returned to his office, and Bill briefly disclosed his conversation with Mike Sears. "So I gather you didn't want the publicity?" Bill said sharply.

"That's correct. Whether I was wrong or right is not for you to judge, but mud sticks, and I do have the University's reputation to

134

consider. Although I did suggest to Ramsey that he be pensioned off and take early retirement," he replied.

"And did he intend to take your advice?"

"Yes. He said he would leave next year in July 2000, although I would have preferred to be rid of him earlier."

"Perhaps if you had you wouldn't have had a murder on your doorstep," Bill suggested.

"I knew the man was disliked, but I must admit I didn't realise just how much," he replied.

"It looks like he's a prime suspect, he hated the man, attacked him both verbally and physically in public, almost killed him in fact," Bill told Josephine.

"Yes, he's a suspect, I agree with you there, and although as yet I haven't met Rob Morton, I would say he's a rather volatile, aggressive person," Josephine noticed.

"Who's to say anyone wouldn't act the same, if they lost someone they cared for," Bill replied.

"The point I'm trying to make Bill, is that this murder appears to be planned down to a tee, with no violence involved, which seems out of character for Morton. Now if Ramsey had been beaten, stabbed, even ploughed down by a car, I would say that method would point to Morton," Josephine explained.

"Let's go and visit him, and hear his side of the story," Bill proposed.

"What we need to determine are his whereabouts between say ten a.m. and two p.m. Even though the door to the lecture room was locked at approximately midday, the probability is that the murderer took Ramsey's mobile phone and insulin earlier, and that the smashed car window was also part of the plan," Josephine told him.

"It could always be a student in his class," Bill suggested.

"Yes, but it would be difficult to remove those things from his briefcase, in front of the entire class without someone seeing," she replied.

* * *

Jack answered the phone in his flat to find it was Rob.

"I've told you not to keep phoning the flat."

"Never mind that," Rob said in an agitated voice. "The police are coming to see me!"

"Well, so what, it's to be expected, they've got nothing on you. Just keep calm. You know in each case we're all suspects, if the police are any good at their job, they'll realise that more or less right away, well after a few enquiries at least. They've probably decided Ramsey's killer would have to be in the vicinity of the University most of the morning, to remove his mobile, and insulin, and then lock the door, and you were miles away at the time. Gary has carried out his instructions, and hasn't panicked," Jack reassured him.

"He'd bloody well panic if the police were on his back," Rob shouted down the phone.

"Look, if you don't keep calm, you'll blow it. I've told you it's obvious they will want to speak to you. Be honest, tell them you hated the guy. Your alibi will clear you, no sweat. Anyway the bastard's dead. You've got revenge, that's what you wanted wasn't it?"

"Well… Yes…" Rob uttered.

"Stay cool, I'll meet you in the Fox and Hounds on Friday," Jack told him. "What if they are following me?"

"Just relax, I'll see you later," Jack said and hung up.

Jack put down the phone. *A bloody perfectly planned murder. Gary who I was worried about carries it out without a hitch, and now Rob's getting panicky and there's two more to go yet.*

* * *

Josephine and Bill sat in Rob's flat above the pub where he worked.

"I suppose you've gathered why we need to speak to you?" Josephine began.

"Yes, well it's all over the University, what's happened," Rob replied.

"I'm so sorry about your girlfriend," Josephine sympathised.

God she seems like a soft touch, unless it's all a con, he thought. He came to the conclusion that they must have spoken to someone about Claire, and knew all the details of her death, so decided to tell the truth about Claire and Ramsey.

"Yes… I mean, she was beating the habit, I'd supported her from the start, and I wanted to marry her. She was so clever, but the drugs were ruining her life."

"But was she really coming off them, I mean I know Ramsey wasn't the best of tutors…" Bill began.

"She killed herself because of him," Rob announced angrily.

138

"But she didn't leave a note, not even to you, saying why she'd committed suicide, if she had," Josephine remarked.

"She told me what a hell life was, how he laid into her at almost every lecture, and she felt a failure. Perhaps I should have realised and not left her alone..." Rob said as his eyes filled with tears.

"We know all about the assault," Josephine told him.

"Yes and my only regret is that I didn't kill him, but they pulled me off!"

"How come you never went back and finished him off at a later date then," Bill asked, "I mean if you hated him that much..."

"I spoke to Claire's mum after the funeral, and more or less said what I wanted to do. She said I'd be caught, and then my life would be ruined, and that Claire wouldn't have wanted that. What she said sort of made sense, so I decided to just leave it," Rob explained.

Be honest and keep calm. Jack's words went through his head. "But there are times when I wished I had killed him."

"Well, now someone's done it for you, so perhaps you weren't the only person Ramsey had crossed. Now can you tell us your whereabouts on Thursday twenty-first October, say between nine a.m. and two p.m.?"

Don't answer the questions too quickly, as it sounds as if your alibi was planned, that's what Jack said.

"A week last Thursday, I don't know where I was," he replied trying to sound vague "At the pub where I work I suppose," he looked a little confused. "Oh hang on, I forgot... I was at my sister's in St Ives, I caught the coach down there."

"Do you still have the tickets?" Bill asked.

"No, I never keep tickets, I went on Tuesday with a friend, I suppose I could ask him if he's got his but I doubt it."

"So let's get this straight," Josephine began, "You went to your sister's at St Ives on Tuesday nineteenth October, two days before his death, so I take it you were there on the day Ramsey died?"

"Yes, with my mate and sister," he replied.

"And I suppose they can confirm this can they?"

"I don't see why not, I stayed there, till Saturday twenty-third, and we got the coach back in the afternoon."

"Right then, if it checks out, and they

140

confirm what you've told us, then I'd say it's your lucky day," Bill said a little condescendingly.

Rob's heart, which had been thumping away, began to slow down a little.

"We'll need both your friend's and sister's addresses," Bill continued.

"No problem, I'll write them down for you."

After they had left, Bill turned to Josephine. " Well, that's convenient, if it all checks out."

"It probably will," Josephine said, "But we'll go through all the procedures with a fine tooth comb."

"If he'd have been anywhere in the vicinity he'd have been a suspect," Bill remarked.

"Lucky for him he wasn't," she replied.

"You said that almost as if you've sticking up for him, he seems a bit of a tough nut to me," Bill observed.

"I agree he lost his rag. Who knows? Maybe he would have ended up killing Ramsey or seriously injuring him, if he hadn't been dragged off. But Ramsey's murder seems entirely different, I'd say it's obvious he's upset a few people, so there is probably more than one suspect."

Two days later Rob's sister and friend confirmed his alibi, and it seemed he was in the clear.

"God, it was a lot easier than I thought it would be," he told Jack and Gary.

"I told you that they couldn't connect you, even if you'd attacked or threatened Ramsey a hundred times beforehand. You were miles away, and there's no way they can get round that," Jack said with grim satisifaction

"You're a clever bastard, Jack! Ramsey dead, Claire avenged, and I'm in the clear. I must admit, I'm impressed!"

"I'm the one who ought to be worried— it's me who took the chances," Gary told them.

Jack looked at him.

"I reduced your chances to a minimum, no one saw you go into the staff room, or lock the door to the science lab, yours was the easiest crime of them all."

"I've just thought," Rob began anxiously. "I've got mine to do yet, getting rid of Miranda, so there's no way I'm out of the woods."

"Well it's got to be done, and I have to dispose of Tony Mulligan. You're okay now

Gary, so try and relax, and Rob, don't come anywhere near the flat, you never know who you might bump into," Jack warned him.

Chapter 11

WHEN JOSEPHINE ARRIVED HOME, the moment she entered her hallway, she was greeted by the smell of exotic spices as they wafted through the air. She made her way to the kitchen.

"That smells inviting," she remarked.

"I'm cooking us a curry," Andrew told her.

"This is a welcome surprise, in fact I didn't expect you back till later," she said glancing at her watch. "I've had such an awful day and I was wondering what I should do us for a meal."

"You sit down, and put your feet up. I've put some cans of lager in the fridge, I thought it would be better than wine, to cool us down."

"It's not going to be that hot is it Andrew?"

"Well I may have been a little heavy with the curry powder," he confessed. Josephine opened the fridge and poured herself a lager. "I'm sure it will be delicious," she lied, as she sat on the kitchen stool next to him, while he continued to cook.

"Why don't you go into the lounge?" he suggested.

"No I'm fine here while you concoct this masterpiece."

"How's the case going?" he asked as he poured Basmati rice into a saucepan of boiling water.

"By all accounts, this Ramsey wasn't a popular man, in fact I haven't spoken to one person who liked him, although the Dean said he was good at his job," she took a drink of her lager, "No, I haven't put that right. He knew his subject, but wasn't a good tutor, as he couldn't relate to his students."

"Then I'd say he was no good. It doesn't matter how much knowledge you have if you can't communicate with people, and pass it on in a way they can understand."

"I see your point, I remember at school and college, some teachers would make the lesson so interesting, a real pleasure. Others were such a bore, you could never understand *what* they were rambling on about, no matter how hard you tried. Anyway *I'm* rambling now. Going back to Ramsey, the only suspect who had a grudge against him happened to be miles away at the time of his death."

"What sort of grudge?" Andrew inquired.

"It was more than a grudge, I used the wrong word. His girlfriend had taken an

146

overdose of drugs and died, he was convinced Ramsey was to blame, he told her she was useless, would never get her degree, that sort of thing."

"If I had a pound for every time a tutor said that to me, I'd be a rich man," Andrew told her.

"Yet look at you now, an eminent forensic psychologist," Josephine teased. "Seriously though, Rob Morton, her boyfriend, was convinced she was really kicking the habit, but she couldn't handle his criticism. Rob attacked and threatened Ramsey in public, and accused him of murdering her."

"Sounds a volatile young man, still many people might do the same under the circumstances," Andrew said as he stirred the rice.

"If Ramsey had suffered a more violent death, I would have said it pointed to Rob Morton. But as far as we know this killer just managed to obtain a key for the room Ramsey was lecturing in and locked him in there. We think the killer removed his mobile phone and insulin, which were his two lifelines. Unfortunately for Ramsey the building where he was lecturing was situated in a very quite spot, so no-one heard him."

"A murder with no violence, or physical contact: in fact, very well planned," Andrew announced.

"OK, off the record, can you give me a profile of what sort of person we should be looking for?"

"Well, as you say, even if Rob hadn't got an alibi, it doesn't appear to be his sort of murder. Since he was so pent-up emotionally, due to the loss of a loved one, I doubt he'd be calm or logical enough to plan this kind of murder."

"The murderer would have had to get into the caretaker's office, possibly the day before and remove the key to the room and have a duplicate made. The insulin and mobile phone may have been removed while he was looking at his car, which may or may not have been smashed by the assailant. I think that would probably be an awkward thing to do without being noticed, then they'd have to go up to the new wing and lock the door. I suppose that would have had to be after all the students had left, because Ramsey's killer couldn't risk the chance of someone seeing them. Unless they were hiding somewhere close by, which is more feasible," Josephine told him.

"It sounds to me like the killer had a busy day, and they didn't appear to have attracted attention to themselves, still I suppose the university is so busy, they'd just mill in with the crowds," Andrew observed.

"I suppose if Ramsey was disliked by a lot of people, there may be more than one person involved," she suggested.

"How do you mean?" Andrew looked confused.

"Well you know, say one could smash his car window, while the other removed the things from his briefcase, although it's all pure conjecture."

"Mmm, possible, but not likely. If people decide to take a life they would probably do it alone. I see your point though; an easy crime in the sense of no violence or struggle, but everything would have to fit in the plan like a jigsaw. The person who smashed the car window may have no knowledge of the murder."

"Well, it would be a lucky coincidence for whoever took the insulin and mobile, and I don't really believe in coincidence where murder's concerned."

"Neither do I," Josephine agreed. "Anyway, enough talk. I'm starving!"

As they started to eat their curry Josephine grabbed her lager and took a gulp.

"If I was boring you with the case, Andrew you should have told me to shut up, not try and burn my tongue off!"

Chapter 12

JACK HAD TOLD GARY to arrange to see three friends on the night in question.

"Meet them at about eight or thereabouts, and ideally stay with them till the early hours of the next day. Suggest a night-club, curry, anything to stay out late," he'd told him.

Gary had looked doubtful, "I don't know if I can" he had replied.

"For heaven's sake, just how difficult can it be for three studs to have a night out," had been Jack's reply when Gary had questioned him about what he should do.

"The hardest part is over for you now, all you have to do is go out and bloody enjoy yourself," were Jack's last words before he left Gary.

Gary had not followed Jack's instructions to the letter and only invited two of his mates, Terry and Pete. At the last minute Pete had telephoned to say he felt rough, and didn't think he'd be able to make it. Gary was in a complete state of panic, thinking that if it was only him and Terry, he might suggest just a few drinks and then home after the pub. But luckily for Gary, Terry brought a girl along, he said Mel was just a friend when he introduced her to Gary. As Terry was getting a round of drinks in, Mel turned to Gary and said, "I hope you didn't mind me turning up, only I know it was supposed to be just a lads' night out."

"No problem at all," he assured her. Terry would never know just how grateful Gary was that he had brought her along.

The evening passed quite quickly and pleasantly. Mel turned out to be quite a laugh, one of the lads in fact, and she knew far more crude jokes than Gary or Terry. As they were leaving the pub, Gary looked at his watch; it was only twenty past eleven.

"Fancy going on somewhere?" he asked quite casually, although his heart was pounding, as his stomach churned.

"No I'm whacked and I've got to be at work early," Terry told him.

"What about you Mel?"

"Well I'm easy, anything in mind?"

"I know a curry house where they do a great Balti," he suggested.

"I'm a bit short of cash," Mel added. Being one of the lads she was always prepared to pay her way.

"My treat, I'm flush this week," Gary announced.

Terry, who had secretly fancied Mel, although he hadn't admitted that to Gary or Mel for that matter, became a bit jealous. He thought Gary had taken a shine to Mel, and was trying to muscle in.

Oh I see, I go home, they go for a curry and he ends up in bed with Mel ,Terry thought to himself.

"Well, if it's your treat mate, I'm game," he said, expecting Gary to put him off so he could be alone with Mel. Which in fact was the furthest thing from Gary's mind.

"That's great mate, the more the merrier, and it's only a short walk from here," he said with his arm around Terry's shoulder. He'd never been so relieved in his life.

He really seems pleased that I'm coming, maybe he doesn't fancy Mel after all Terry thought.

Mel hadn't the faintest idea what was going on in the minds of the two young men she was spending the evening with. Gary needed her along with Terry, purely as an alibi, and Terry wanted to get her into bed. The one thing she did notice in the curry house was that they both seemed in a good mood.

They all left the Indian restaurant at about one thirty in the morning and made their way back home; all that was on Gary's mind was

153

that he wondered if Jack had carried out his task successfully.

Jack had been watching Tony Mulligan's local pub, the White Hart for the past two weeks. He had taken the details of the days he went there, what time he would usually leave, and which nights he'd most likely be alone. Unfortunately, after Jack had completed his survey, the proprietor banned Mulligan from the pub for being drunk and disorderly. The advantage for Jack about that particular pub was that even though Mulligan had no qualms about drinking and driving, the White Hart was in walking distance from his home, or in his case staggering distance. Jack had become very frustrated and anxious because there was no pattern to Mulligan's drinking venues. He'd visited many different places but didn't seem to stick to any of them. Perhaps he was hoping to pal up with some other alcoholic.

After a week, much to Jack's relief, Mulligan found a pub that suited him, and it was reasonably close to where he lived. The only snag was that some evenings Mulligan would walk part of the way home with a fellow drinker. On this particular evening, his companion had not turned up, so if Mulligan did leave the pub alone, Jack decided to attack either in the rear car park or the alleyway Mulligan would walk through on his way home. If Mulligan did happen to leave with someone, Jack would just wait till they parted company. If, for some reason, Jack didn't succeed tonight, then Gary would have to arrange an alibi for another night.

Jack however was in luck, for despite the fact Mulligan had left the pub obviously the worse for drink and with his companion, they started to argue in the car park. The argument escalated to a near fight and Jack saw Mulligan's drinking companion push Mulligan into a nearby parked car, causing him to bang his head. Jack stood in the shadows and watched although they were both so drunk, they probably wouldn't have noticed him anyway.

"Well you can piss off, you bastard! That's the last time you'll get a drink off me," his companion shouted before staggering off, leaving Mulligan on the ground.

Jack could have finished him off there and then, but decided it was a bit too risky, as the car park was partly lit, and the owner of the car may have possibly turned up.

After a few minutes, Mulligan got slowly to his feet, staggering slightly and made his way out of the car park and along the alley.

It couldn't be easier, the state he's in, Jack thought.

He walked up behind him, holding a cricket bat which was covered with a black bin liner. Jack wore trainers so he hardly made a sound as he approached Mulligan. It was odd how Mulligan sensed there was someone behind him, even in his inebriated state.

"So you've come back to help me Mac..." he said incoherently as he half turned his head.

Before Mulligan had chance to mumble anything further, Jack struck him across the side of the head with such force he heard Mulligan's skull crack.

Mulligan fell to the ground without making a sound, not even a whimper or a moan of pain. Jack thought he may have killed him outright, with just one blow, but he wasn't prepared to take any chances. As he lay motionless, he continued to smash his head and face with the bat, as blood oozed out over the pavement. When Jack was certain he was dead he put the cricket bat that was covered, but dripping with blood, into another black bin liner, that he had rolled up in his pocket and walked away very quickly.

Because Mulligan hadn't made a sound, Jack felt he'd disturbed no-one, as no house lights had been turned on, along the road. As he reached the end of the road and was just about to turn the corner he was suddenly confronted by a huge Alsatian, which started barking at him. He didn't know whether to hit the dog with the bat, or make a run for it, and decided on the latter as he sprinted down the road.

Oh shit, I just don't believe this! It all went off like a dream, and now this bloody dog's after me, he thought.

After about twenty yards or so, it appeared the dog had given up his chase, so Jack stopped running and leant up against a tree, trying to catch his breath. Even though he was quite fit, the fact he'd been carrying the heavy bat had hampered his speed. But he realised to drop it along the road or dispose of it over someone's fence into the garden would be disastrous, like handing the police the murder weapon on a plate.

He stopped to listen for a while, the barking had ceased, and he couldn't hear the scamper of paws, so he decided to just walk away quietly. Suddenly as if out of nowhere the dog sprung out, knocking Jack to the ground. The animal was no longer barking, just growling viciously, as his razor sharp teeth bit into Jack's leg just above his ankle. The pain was excruciating, but Jack knew if he shouted out in agony, it would disturb the neighbours.

Oh fuck! I can't get caught now he thought as he groaned.

The dog was determined he wasn't going to let go of Jack's leg. As he fell, Jack had dropped the bat, and it was just out of his reach, as he lay sprawled on the pavement. He knew he would have to try and move his leg, but it felt like it was being crushed in a vice, and by doing so he could incur further injury, but he knew that somehow he had to get the bat.

For some reason, the dog momentarily loosened his grip, and Jack had a split second chance. He rolled over on to his left side and made a desperate attempt to reach the bat, its being wrapped in a bin liner made it more difficult, but he pulled it towards him with all his strength. From a sitting position he swung the bat and caught the dog on the side of its head; the dog immediately loosened its grip, and Jack's leg became free, as the dog whimpered in pain and retreated.

Up until then Jack had remained calm, unnaturally so, considering he had just committed a brutal and bloody murder and been attacked by a mad animal. But now he found himself shaking uncontrollably, as the sweat rolled down his face. He looked down at his leg, but due to the darkness he could not see any blood, and his torn jeans didn't seem wet, so he hoped the beast hadn't drawn blood, as the last thing he needed was traces of his blood anywhere near the scene of the crime.

The bat suddenly seemed as heavy as lead, and he felt he would collapse at any moment, but somehow he managed to make it back home on foot, as he couldn't risk coming in his own car, or catching a taxi home.

When he arrived back he staggered up the stairs to his flat and poured himself a large brandy.

Three glasses later he was still shaking.

Chapter 13

BILL AND JOSEPHINE sat in her office going through the details of Paul Ramsey's murder. Bill lit a cigarette, much to Josephine's annoyance, as she had given them up for almost a year, but she knew he'd been feeling tense lately, so decided not to have a moan at him.

"We've got to get a result on this one, as much for my self confidence, as anything else," she sighed.

"What, like having the Chief breathing down our necks, or the fact it looks bad for the department?" he asked before taking another drag of his cigarette. Josephine was tempted to take it from his hand and smoke it herself, she felt so tense.

"I've gone through the forensic report on the body with Brian Morrison, and as far as fibres, etc, from the assailant, there's nothing to go on."

"How did you get on with the report from Ramsey's GP?" Bill asked.

"It seems he was diagnosed with diabetes four years ago, at the age of forty-four. Some cases can be treated with tablets, but because his case was more severe, he had to have injections daily. Apparently at the beginning of a patient's diagnosis, it's sometimes difficult to get the balance of the drugs and insulin just right. A strict diet has to be followed, and at the start of treatment, people can still faint and collapse. But once its regulated, it can be more or less plain sailing," Josephine enlightened him.

"I think it must have been something he didn't discuss," Bill observed, "as hardly any of the staff or students knew he was a diabetic. Maybe he was embarrassed, although it is a reasonably common and treatable complaint nowadays."

"He seemed a very private person, but the murderer obviously knew of his diabetes," Josephine added.

"He may have been private, but he had nasty streak, to have treated Claire the way he did. It's almost a pity Rob Morton had an alibi, he was an obvious candidate for the murder," he said.

"Well a pity for us, but not for him, I was thinking though, since Rob was so cut up about her death, her family must have felt the same grudge against Ramsey, it's possible there could be a motive there," Josephine suggested.

162

"I see your point, but would a member of her family know the lay-out of the university and the details of Ramsey's lectures... Mind you I suppose they could have found out from a fellow student or someone who worked there."

"But wouldn't that point the finger at them, I mean if they started asking questions around the campus, someone might get suspicious," she replied.

"Perhaps we should speak to Rob Morton again, I know he's in the clear, but he may know other people who also blamed Ramsey for Claire's death, and when we've exhausted that avenue we shall have to look for another motive," Bill concluded.

When Josephine arrived at Torbay Police Department Headquarters the following morning DI Frank Blundell came over to her.

"Hi Josephine how are things?"

"Fine... well that's a lie, I'm having a few problems with a case at the moment. Anyway, what are you doing down here, it's not your neck of the woods?"

DI Blundell was normally based at Brixham.

"Your Chief's called me in about a murder case," he replied.

Suddenly Josephine became anxious and angry, initially thinking that Chief Cunningham had asked DI Blundell to take over her case, which Josephine considered an absolute atrocity since the Chief hadn't even informed her.

In the past, the Chief had sometimes suggested to Josephine that she was becoming emotionally involved in certain cases, but she had always stuck to her guns and eventually would come out on top with an arrest.

"What a damn cheek! He hasn't even discussed it with me," she became very red in the face.

Blundell was just about to speak when she continued, " Okay, we haven't got a result… but it's early days…"

"Hang on a minute, what the hell are you on about? I've been called in about a body found on the roadside just outside Exeter," he informed her.

"Oh… I thought…" Josephine became acutely embarrassed. "I think I may have jumped to the wrong conclusion."

"My thinking entirely," Blundell said smiling. He could see how awkward and uncomfortable Josephine felt and perhaps many in his position would have played on that fact. Blundell, however, was a professional, and had known Josephine for many years. He both liked and respected her.

"Look, I know Chief Cunningham from way back," he began. "He has been known to drop bombshells on people in the past, but in this case he's blameless. They were going to call you in, but since you've got two murders on your plate at the moment, he's asked me in to investigate this one, and I'm sure they are not linked in anyway."

It was Josephine's own uncertainty and insecurity about the case that had caused her to feel everyone else felt the same. She had criticised and accused Frank without any facts.

"I'm sorry Frank... things haven't been going too well... I really shouldn't have..."

"Forget it. Look, do you want to come down with me to see the Chief?" He asked.

"No, it's best if you go alone, I'll maybe catch up with you later and you can fill me in with what's happening."

Josephine went into her office feeling terrible. She knew she would have to put the awkward moment behind her, and concentrate on the case in hand, although she hadn't made much progress. There had been situations and tough cases many times in her past career, but something had always turned up, but she felt this case would be a hard one to crack. The following day DI Frank Blundell called into her office.

"Hi, feeling better?" he asked a little patronisingly. "I've come to run through the details with you."

"There's no need, still I suppose, a fresh outlook on the case, we might be able to help each other," she replied.

"I'm off duty in the next fifteen minutes," Frank said glancing at his watch. "Fancy a drink?"

"Okay but I could do with some food, I've hardly eaten today," she added.

Half an hour or so later they were sitting in a nearby pub that Josephine frequented. Frank bought a bottle of wine, and Josephine ordered two chilli con carnés with rice, and paid for them at the counter.

"Come on then, spill the beans, I want to hear about your two cases," Frank began as they sat down. Josephine acquainted him with the facts to date about the murders of

Sophie Bryan and Paul Ramsey.

"I mean we've explored every avenue with Sophie, and couldn't find any possible motive, even though we've spoken to family, friends colleagues, old boyfriends. I know it sounds corny but she did appear to be the girl that everyone loved. I felt awful having to tell her parents we'd come to a standstill.

"If only I'd had some lead, something to go on. I could have given them some sort of hope, but there was nothing. The next line of enquiry was that it was some madman, and that she was just at the wrong place at the wrong time, but again, a dead end. Then with Ramsey's case, the one possible suspect, who had a convincingly strong reason to kill him, had a cast-iron alibi. I tell you Frank, I'm losing it."

"Rubbish! The best detective in the world needs some sort of a lead or at least something substantial to go on. Nobody could have done any better," he assured her.

"I know in Paul Ramsey's case there we're no witnesses and in Sophie Bryan's there were literally hundreds of people about, but they were all obsessed with the eclipse, so no-one really noticed anything. Anyway I've rattled on enough, what about your case?"

"In a nutshell; Tony Mulligan, beaten to a pulp, severe head injuries."

"Weapon?" she enquired.

"All we can tell at the moment is that it was a heavy object, possibly smooth edged, until forensics or the lab come up with more information. The body was found two hundred yards or so from the Red Lion pub".

"Was it his local?"

"Well, if you could call it that, apparently he'd been barred from one or two pubs. When we ran his details through the computer we found he'd been convicted for drink driving."

"Oh well, it comes to us all sooner or later," Josephine said as she took a drink of her wine. Just at that moment the waiter came over to the table with their meals; after he had left, Frank continued.

"It was rather more than that I'm afraid. He had killed a girl of seventeen, and been sentenced to three years, but apparently he was released after serving just two, for good behaviour, and he'd even been caught driving again with no licence. I know you shouldn't talk ill of the dead, but in my opinion, they should have locked him up and thrown away the key. Drink driving that causes death is murder in my book, and the sentences are far too short."

"I agree with you Frank and it's the families I feel for, knowing that whoever was responsible for a loved one's death is walking around as free as a bird after just two years or so," Josephine replied.

"Going back to your case, even though both victims were connected to the university I don't believed they are linked in any way."

"No, neither do I, it's just that there seems to be a lot of murders on my patch. Bill always jokes that I'm jinxed."

"How is Bill, I haven't seen him in ages?" Frank asked.

"You know Bill—he never changes. Still we've got a good working relationship, although we are always taking the mickey out of each other. We've come through a lot together over the past few years and, apart from a marriage partner, he's one of the closest people to me," she announced. Frank raised his eyebrows in a fanciful manner and winked; Josephine knew what he was thinking.

"Before you say a word, it's strictly a working relationship, he's just like a big brother, except that I'm older than he is," she confessed.

"You don't look it; you're wearing well," he

noticed as he looked at a somewhat tired, but still attractive women, with short blonde hair, that was streaked with grey and soft blue eyes.

"Thanks for the compliment, I don't get many at my age," she admitted. "The only problem with Bill is, he's putting on weight."

"Aren't we all?" Frank said tapping a slightly rounded stomach.

"Seriously though, how's life treating you?" Frank asked.

"Not that it's any of your business," she began as she smiled teasingly. "I suppose you know Tom and I are divorced?"

"Yes, it was common knowledge throughout the department."

"I'm seeing Andrew Blythe now, the forensic psychologist, I believe you've worked with him in the past."

"Is it serious?"

"I am afraid so, he's been my rock for the past two years, I couldn't have survived without him," she confessed.

"I can hardly believe this is Detective Inspector Josephine Blake talking, who never relied on anyone if she could possibly avoid it."

"That was the younger, possibly more

confident version, not the middle-aged slightly insecure one you're looking at now."

"I don't believe a word of it," Frank said, knocking back the remainder of his wine. "So what's the next step?"

"Marriage, if Andrew has his way."

"And will he?"

"Mind your own business and eat your chilli," she said smiling.

Chapter 14

JACK ARRANGED TO MEET Rob and Gary at a country pub some five miles away. They had both moaned it was too far out, but Jack was adamant. They were huddled up on three wooden stools around a rustic looking table in the corner. A large log fire crackled away in the nearby fireplace. The pub was homely and comfortable, although the seating left a lot to be desired. The surroundings were calm and cosy, but their minds were in turmoil.

"I can't understand why they came to see me again," Rob began nervously.

"I mean my alibi checked out, and that police woman… er, DI Blake, I think her name was. Well at first she seemed okay, quite sympathetic in fact, about me losing Claire."

"Look don't go getting all soft on me. It's them and us, remember, and most coppers are pigs anyway," Jack said sharply.

"Oh I don't know," Gary interrupted, "they were really good when Isabella was killed."

"For God's sake have you forgotten, two of us have committed murder, and Rob's still got his treat to come," Jack said sarcastically "Believe me, if they lock us away for the next fifteen years, you won't like them then. This bird might seem okay on the surface, but my bet is she's as hard as nails. All they're interested in is getting a result. If she thinks the gentle approach will get you to open up, then she'll use it, and then sting you like a deadly female scorpion."

"Look, you got us into this situation, and now you're making us scared shitless," Gary told him.

"Look, you've both got your retribution. Ramsey's dead, and so's Mulligan, but that bloody bitch Miranda is still walking about. It was my plan, and I'm the only one was hasn't benefitted from it as yet."

"You will, I'll do my bit, I'm not going back on my word," Rob assured him.

"I know you're damn well not," Jack said with malice. "Look, let's talk this through sensibly. They've got nothing on you Rob, you were a suspect, and now you're off the list, so what exactly did they want?"

"They just needed to know if I thought any of Claire's family or friends would want her death avenged and did I know of any other enemies of Ramsey's," Rob explained.

"So they didn't accuse you, or point the finger," Jack asked.

"No, they were okay."

"So why the fuck are you panicking? They are only doing their job, let's face it Ramsey was a shit and a loner, no real family. He's probably done the dirty and criticised more people than Claire, but they only know about her, so you being her boyfriend it's natural they should want to talk to you again. In fact it would have been odd, if they hadn't approached you. We've got to keep calm, things are going to plan."

"Have the police contacted you yet Gary?" Rob asked.

"No, still I suppose they may in a day or so," he replied.

"How did you kill him?" Rob asked Jack.

"It's safer if you don't know, the police will give Gary the details if they contact him, and if he accidentally let something out he wasn't supposed to know, it could prove dangerous. Anyway it should be in the local papers."

"I wish they would hurry up and contact me, so I could get the ordeal over and done with," Gary told them both.

"Look they've got to run his details though the police computer. Even if they know he killed your sister, they may look closer to home to start with, his family, friends, enemies, then

175

if they can't find any motive, they will start to look further afield. Then they may contact you or your dad. What time did you leave your mates?"

"Oh about one thirty," Gary informed him.

"That's fine, you're sorted. I'd say he died about eleven thirty, so there's no problem there," Jack assured him. Rob and Gary started to relax, and the strained, tense expressions on their faces disappeared, Gary went to the bar and ordered another three pints of lager. As he returned and put them on the table Jack began. "Look, when I planned all this, I knew there may be hitches along the way, but I knew they'd only be minor. All that's left to do is for you Rob, to follow my instructions for Miranda. I'll sort out my alibi when we have a future date planned and then it will all be over."

"Yes, well, I'd like to get it over and done with as soon as possible, and yet you've given me no instructions as yet," Rob said.

"The final details haven't been sorted out yet, my plan has to be perfect, as I can't risk any mistakes that would put either of us in jeopardy; you'll just have to trust me, and wait until I'm ready. We've got to support and trust one another one hundred percent, and then there's nothing to worry about."

"We're with you all the way," Gary stated.

"Yeah, to the hilt," Rob added.

"Right then," Jack said as he raised his glass. "To us, and the next crime," he said quietly, so the other customers in the pub couldn't overhear him.

DI Frank Blundell and his team were going through the normal procedures of the murder enquiry. It appeared that, although Tony Mulligan was still with his wife, they didn't get on. She was sick of the drunkenness and violence that she'd had to endure over the years. It was almost a relief for her when he was imprisoned, but even then she had to suffer abuse from her neighbours, as well as anonymous phone calls and letters, saying he was a murderer, and she was no better. The few friends they had turned against them; perhaps they felt sorry for Kathy Mulligan, but there was no way they wanted to be associated with Mulligan or his family. The whole family was ashamed when they read the tragic accounts in the local newspapers, how a lovely young girl had been, as one paper put it, "Ploughed down in the prime of her life." Mulligan's son was so ashamed and disgusted he had left home, but had recently been re-united with his mother on hearing about his father's death. The neighbours in the road where his body was found had been interviewed at length, but no one had seen anything, only a few said they heard a dog barking. The area had been searched thoroughly but no weapon had been found. The man who had been drinking with Tony Mulligan in the pub and had a scuffle with him in the car park had been interviewed. According to the bar staff and other customers at the time he was hardly in a fit state to walk home, let alone batter someone to death. Unfortunately Kathy Mulligan had destroyed all the malicious letters, so they couldn't be examined in the hope they may have had some connection with his murder, even though they had been sent to her some two years previously.

Chapter 15

NEIL DOWNES called to his Alsatian, Rex. "Here boy, dinnertime!" he shouted as he placed the bowl of dog food on the kitchen floor. Usually the dog would demolish the contents of his bowl in less than a minute, but he just stood there looking at the food before walking away. Neil followed his pet into the lounge.

"That's not like you boy," he said as he patted the animal's head.

Suddenly the dog whimpered and moved away. Neil gently held him by the collar, and noticed a patch of dry blood behind the dog's ear. Rex broke away and went into his dog basket in the kitchen, where he stayed during the day. He curled up like the wounded animal he was. As Neil went up to the basket he noticed a jagged piece of blue denim material that was speckled in dark red.

"Have you been a naughty boy again? No wonder you got a bump on the head," Neil said to the dog, as if he were talking to a naughty child who understood every word he was saying. Since Neil's wife had died, and his son had left home, Rex was his only companion, and he adored his dog. The Alsatian in the past had gone to bite people, but luckily Neil had always been there to pull him away, just in the nick of time. His biggest worry was that one of these days, he wouldn't be there and Rex would bite someone, and have to be put down. The thought of losing his pet was dreadful. He removed the piece of cloth and examined it closely; it appeared to be from a trouser leg, and the spots looked like blood. Neil felt his worst fears had been confirmed. He picked it up and took it outside to the dustbin.

Well that's the evidence gone, now let's clean you up, he thought, *no-one's been knocking at my door complaining they had been bitten as yet, so if and when they do I'll just plead ignorance and say it must have been some other dog.*

He got a bowl of warm water, and cotton wool and set about cleaning the dog's wound.

After completing their house to house enquiries the police were still searching the road where the body was discovered. On DI Blundell's instructions, they were to search any dustbins that were situated at the front of the houses on the slim chance the assailant may have disposed of the weapon locally. As one PC was looking systematically through each dustbin, he lifted the lid of the one at number thirty-four Albert Road and started to sift through the contents. He happened to come across a piece of torn denim covered in what appeared to be blood.

Mmm—might be nothing. Still you never know, the DI did say bag anything you might think is important, he thought as he carefully removed it and placed it into a clear plastic bag.

He was unsure whether to knock on the door of number thirty-four and tell the occupant of his findings, but decided against it till he'd checked with Sergeant Myers, who was in charge of the team that was searching the vicinity.

Two days later the piece of fabric was being examined by forensics, and the blood group AB was a perfect match to the victim's. Their findings were passed on to DI Frank Blundell.

"Well, the victim Mulligan was wearing black cord trousers at the time of his death so how that piece of fabric happens to have his blood on it is a mystery at this stage. I think we'll go and see the occupant of the house. The dustbin is at the front of the house, so it's quite possible anyone could have put it in there," Frank told his sergeant. When the police car pulled up outside Neil Downes' house and three officers alighted, two of them in uniform and one in plain clothes, he was shocked.

Surely if Rex had bitten someone they would only send a constable to the house. How come there are three of them? He became very nervous and agitated.

"What have you done?" he said looking at the dog's face.

As he answered the door Frank showed his ID.

"I'm DI Blundell," he began, "and these are two officers from my station."

"Er… Yes…" Downes sounded vague.

"Can we come in for a moment?"

"Yes of course," he replied showing them into the lounge.

"Fine dog," Frank noticed looking at Rex.

"I think so."

"I used to be a police dog handler, before I joined CID," he explained.

"What's all this about?" Downes asked.

"I take it you know a vicious attack

182

resulting in a murder enquiry took place in your road a few nights ago," Frank began.

"Yes you could hardly not know, with all the police activity and part of the road being cordoned off," he replied.

"Well, when my officers were searching the area, this was found in your dustbin," he said, showing him the piece of fabric that had he carefully removed from its plastic bag with tweezers.

"What is it?" Downes asked pretending to be ignorant.

"A piece of material from, we believe, a pair of denim jeans, but more to the point, the blood on it is a perfect match to the victim, a Mr Mulligan."

"Oh..." he said looking shocked. "Only I thought..." he never finished his sentence.

"Yes go on... what did you think Mr Downes?" Frank asked.

"Nothing," he said, "I was just thinking out loud."

"So have you any idea how it came to be in your dustbin?"

"No," he replied. "Maybe someone else put it in there."

He became very red in the face, and said shakily.

"I don't know why you're asking me all this…"

He's hiding something, Frank thought to himself.

"Perhaps you'd like to come down to the station for questioning," Frank suggested.

"Why? I've done nothing," he uttered.

"Some neighbours said they heard a dog barking on the night of the murder, did you hear anything?"

"No!" Downes replied.

"Was your dog barking?"

"No he was in the house with me, I was watching TV," he lied.

"Oh, so he doesn't sleep outside," Frank asked as he noticed the kennel on the patio outside.

As much as Neil Downes loved his dog, he knew he'd have to come clean, even though it might mean that the dog would have to be destroyed.

"Look, I'll tell you the truth," he began, "I found the piece of denim in the dog's basket a few days ago, and I threw it in the dustbin."

"Didn't it occur to you that it may be linked to the murder?" Frank asked.

"Well no," he answered as he lit a cigarette. "Rex has been known to go for people in the

184

past, although I've always managed to restrain him. He did get out a few nights ago and when I saw the denim covered in blood, I guessed it might be part of a trouser leg. I thought he'd bitten someone, he had blood behind his ear, and when I washed it off I noticed he had a large painful lump."

"How did you know it was painful, did he tell you?" one officer said sarcastically.

"No, but he whined in pain, God, I know my dog better than anyone does," he replied tersely.

"Please continue," Blundell said looking sternly at the PC.

"I thought whoever he had attacked, had hit him in self-defence, you see if they complain, and it can be proven, Rex will have to be destroyed," his eyes filled with tears. "Since my wife died, he's all I have left, I couldn't bear to lose him."

"Look Mr Downes, I have two dogs of my own, so I know how you feel, but since some of your neighbours heard a dog barking, it's possible that your dog attacked the murderer," Frank explained.

"So why would the victim's blood be on the denim?" Downes asked.

"Well, we can't go into detail at the moment,

but since no dog's hairs have been found on the victim's body, it suggests Rex wasn't anywhere near Tony Mulligan. This bump on the dog's head I take it is recent, so he could have been struck by the assailant, possibly with the same weapon he used to kill Mulligan."

"So no-one's complained to you about being attacked by a dog?"

"On the contrary, it's quite possible that Rex has actually bitten the murderer, far from being put down, I would say your dog's a bit of a hero," Frank said patting the animal on the head.

Neil Downes beamed with pride as he looked over at Rex.

In the incident room DI Blundell was going through the details with his investigation team.

"According to forensics," he began, "The injuries that Mulligan sustained could have sprayed blood onto the assailant's clothing. Since the piece of torn denim does not belong to Mulligan's clothing, it's more than likely that the dog attacked the murderer as he was leaving the scene of the crime. This is only a theory, but it's possible the murderer struck the dog with the same weapon he used to murder Mulligan. I believe the denim to be a torn piece from the jeans the murderer was wearing at the time. So, I'd say the person we are looking for would have bite marks to his ankle or lower leg area, and since there is no other blood type on the denim, it appears the dog didn't bite the assailant deep enough to draw blood."

After he had given them certain instructions the briefing ended.

Later that day Frank informed Josephine of his progress.

"Well at least you've got something to go on, which is more than I can say, even if it did come from a dumb animal," she said a little bitterly.

"Don't knock dogs, they are far more intelligent than people think," Frank told her.

"I know, I'm sorry Frank, just jealous I suppose, ignore me, anything else come up?"

"Well, I am going to see the father of the girl that Mulligan killed, a Mr Kennedy. Although I've no actual suspects to see as such."

"Surely he's not a suspect?" Josephine asked. "I know he's lost his daughter but..."

"Well how would you feel if some drunk ploughed Jessica down and left her to die, served half his sentence and was walking round as free as a bird, and was still drinking and driving, when disqualified and endangering other lives?" he asked.

"Point taken," she replied.

"In fact some people might think whoever got rid of Mulligan, did the world a favour!"

Chapter 16

"SO WHAT DO YOU WANT me to say, I'm not sorry for one minute, I can tell you that. Well, no, that's not strictly true, I can sympathise with Mulligan's family and what they are going through, but apart from that..." Mr Kennedy told DI Blundell. "I felt my world had fallen apart".

Frank walked over to a nearby table, where an arrangement of photographs in silver frames was displayed. The one at the forefront was a picture of the most beautiful girl Frank had ever seen. She had black flowing hair and deep green eyes.

She looks like an angel; I can see why her father is so devastated.

"She was lovely," he said to Mr Kennedy.

"You don't have to tell me that. Our pride and joy, and murdered before her life had really begun. She was training to be a ballet dancer... so gifted... so much grace," his eyes filled with tears.

"I'm so sorry, it must have been awful for you," Frank sympathised.

Mr Kennedy regained his composure.

"It affected my wife worse than anyone, I

had my job, our son Gary went away to university, but she was in the house all day with just her memories."

"Your wife didn't work then?"

"No she had been ill for some years with chronic asthma and angina, but before Isabella died, the doctor had prescribed a new drug, that seemed to be working. But after the accident, Helen just went down hill rapidly. She'd given up her fight to live, you see. There's only me and my son left now, and I don't see him that often, in fact the last time was at his mother's funeral."

"Many would say Mulligan got his just rewards," Frank remarked.

"I did hate him at the time and I wanted him dead, as I feel he's responsible for two deaths, not just Isabella's but my wife's too. Now I think that emptiness has taken the place of the hate I felt. I think the hardest thing to come to terms with is that he felt no remorse. He didn't even come over to me in court and say sorry. When we found out he was driving again, I thought oh no, some other poor family might suffer," he explained.

"I believe in some cases similar to this one, the guilty person is so devastated at taking a life, and too ashamed to approach the victim's family with any sort of condolences. But from what I've learnt of Mulligan, that wasn't the case, he was a thoroughly despicable human being," Frank stated.

Mr Kennedy nodded in agreement but didn't speak.

"I'm sorry I have to ask you this question sir, but can you tell me your whereabouts on Thuirsday 4th November, say between 7 p.m. and midnight?"

"God, am I a suspect?" he asked astounded.

"No, not in my opinion sir, but it's purely procedure I'm afraid."

There are times when I bloody hate this job, he thought.

"If I can remember, I'd say it's the same as every other night of the week. I usually get home about six thirty in the evening, I never used to work that late but there's nothing to come to home for anymore," he began sadly. "I popped something in the microwave for supper, and then I'd sit down with a drink, and watch the box all night, no one to verify that I'm afraid, I suppose I could have done it," he said sarcastically. "Do you know in a macabre sort of way, I wish I had, if only I'd got the guts, at least it would be some sort of revenge for Isabella and Helen."

191

"Well thank you for your time, Mr Kennedy. I'm sorry I had to bring back memories. I know it's no consolation, but there's a few of us at the police department who truly believe he got what he deserved, which is a rather unprofessional statement for an Inspector to make."

"Maybe so, but at least it's an honest one" Mr Kennedy replied.

A few days later Frank told Josephine about his interview with Mr Kennedy.

"Do you know Frank, I really feel for that man, even though I've never met him, it must have been dreadful."

"That's the feminine side coming to the forefront," he told her.

"No it's not!" she snapped.

"Only joking. To be honest, I felt exactly the same," he admitted.

"So he's not involved?"

"I don't think so for one minute, but then I never did, but, since Mulligan had killed his daughter, it was a procedure I had to carry out."

"Daughter and wife dead, son at university, he must be so lonely," Josephine remarked.

"His son does come down from Exeter to stay for the occasional weekend, although he says he hasn't seen him since his wife's funeral."

"Mmm... Exeter University seems to be figuring in a lot of cases in a roundabout way," she noticed.

"How do you mean?"

"Well my first victim killed at the total eclipse, Sophie Bryan, studied there for a year, before leaving the degree course. And as you know, in the case in hand, Ramsey was a tutor there, and now Mr Kennedy's son... I wonder if there's a connection."

"Josephine, I think you're clutching at straws, there are thousands of people associated with the place, it's purely coincidence."

"I told Andrew the other day, I don't believe in coincidence where murder is concerned."

"I suppose I could go back and talk to the son, Gary Kennedy. I mean he's lost both his mother and his sister, so I suppose he's affected as much as his father."

"Yeah, and if he has a dog bite on his leg we're laughing. Josephine this is getting to be a joke."

"Not to me it's not," she said seriously.

"Look Frank, just go and talk to him, what can you lose, it's just an inkling I've got, call it female intuition."

"Okay, just to please you, I will. I'll phone Mr Kennedy and get the address."

"I can't understand it," Gary began. "Nobody from the police has even tried to contact me yet, and Mulligan's been dead ten days. They've been to see dad, and asked him where he was on the night in question; he just said he was in watching TV... God you don't think they suspect him? I couldn't have dad hounded."

"Calm down Gary," Jack told him.

"You knew they would need to speak to him, purely for the fact that Mulligan killed his daughter, it's just normal procedure. Anyway was your dad pleased the bastard got his just desserts?"

"He more or less said nothing could bring Mum or Isabella back, and that he felt indifferent to his death," Gary replied.

"Anyway, if they do come to see you, which they will sooner or later, you can always get Mel and Terry to substantiate your alibi, it's plain sailing."

"If they are going to speak to me, I'd like it over with, I'm really on tenterhooks waiting."

"Apart from your alibi, there's something else in your favour."

"What's that?" Gary asked confused.

"This!" Jack said as he rolled up his trouser leg to show the deep bite marks at the bottom of his left leg.

"What the hell is that?"

"Well, I didn't say anything to you and Rob at the time, but after I'd killed Mulligan, a bloody dog attacked me, when I was running away."

"Did anyone see you?" Rob asked.

"I don't think so, it was so dark, but I bet they heard the dog barking. If the police have got any sense and they do their job right, they might find the piece of denim the bloody beast tore off my jeans."

"Bloody hell Jack," Gary shouted.

"Look, no sweat I've burned them, they were a designer pair as well, cost me a fortune. Anyway what I'm getting at is they might be looking for bite marks on the assailant's legs and yours are fine, which is just an extra thing in your favour, not that you needed it. The cast iron alibi would exonerate you."

"What if they look at your leg?" Gary said.

"Why should they, I'm not connected in any way. But I tell you something, what I arranged for you to do to ensure Ramsey died was a damn sight easier than mine, it was a bloody nightmare. At one stage I thought the animal would tear my leg off or I'd bleed to death, luckily I managed to hit him with the bat I used to kill Mulligan. Still I was cool enough to handle it," Jack boasted.

"I'm sorry to disturb you Mr Kennedy after a long day at work," Frank began.

"Yes what is it?" he asked.

"I was wondering if we could have your son's address?"

"Do you intend to hound *him* now?" he asked bitterly.

"No, as I said before it's just standard procedure," Frank replied.

"Hang on, it's in my book, I will have to fetch it."

A minute or so later, he returned to the phone.

"He's in flat 6 Church Lane… oh no hang on I've forgotten he's no longer at that address… wait a moment."

Frank could hear the rustling of papers

through the receiver "…Number eighteen Stoneford Way, it's a building converted into bedsits, from what Gary told me, though I'm not sure of the flat number."

"That's not a problem, we'll find it, and once again I'm sorry to disturb you."

Frank hung up the phone.

When Gary knew the police were coming to talk to him, he decided not to act too unemotionally. After all he had hated Tony Mulligan, which was a natural response. The man had killed his sister and contributed to his mother's death. To feel no revulsion for the man may appear strange to the police.

"I suppose you know from your father and the various newspaper reports about the brutal murder of Tony Mulligan, the man responsible for your sister's death," DI Blundell began.

"Yes I do," Gary replied. "Whoever killed him did my family a favour. I feel now that he's dead some sort of justice has been done. In fact I'd like to shake the hand of whoever killed him."

Oh, bloody hell, maybe I've gone a bit over the top with that last statement, Gary thought.

DI Frank Blundell expected more vehemence and fury from Gary than his father, as the young tended to be more aggressive and hot-blooded so he wasn't shocked by Gary's declaration.

"Some would say two wrongs don't make a right, but I've spoken to your father, and I can understand your feelings to an extent. I gather your sister's death may have contributed to your mother's demise."

"I'm sure it did," Gary agreed. "Mom hadn't been well for some time, but she just gave up the will to live, and the worst thing was, I understand he was still drinking and driving whilst disqualified. I hope he rots in Hell!"

"I suppose some would say you had as good a reason as anyone to want Mulligan dead," Frank suggested.

"Yes, you could say that, but I didn't kill him."

"Well, we do need to know your whereabouts on the night in question."

Gary was just about to start telling him, when he remembered Jack's words. *Don't forget, stop and think: no one knows where they were and what they were doing at any given time, just off the cuff.*

"What day was that?" Gary asked.

"Thursday the fourth of November, I need to know your whereabouts, say from eight o'clock in the evening onwards," Frank told him.

Gary pretended to think for a few moments, "...So lets see, not last Thursday, but the one before. Let me think... Oh yes... I remember. I went to the pub, and then afterwards for a curry with two friends."

"Can you give me the names of the pub, and the curry house, and also the names of your friends?"

"The pub was the White Swan, and the curry house was in Stoney Lane, I can't remember the name, Tandoori something. I can give you Terry's name and address, but not Mel's, the girl he brought with him, she's his friend, and I don't know her that well."

When Frank had taken down all the information he needed he said, " That's all for now then Mr Kennedy, if it all checks out, I doubt you'll be hearing from me again."

Phew, thank God for that, Gary thought.

Just as he was about to leave Frank said, Suddenly "Oh by the way, would you roll up your trouser legs?"

Gary did so immediately, without

questioning why he had to do so, or even looking vague in any way, which he considered a mistake.

Frank looked at the unmarked, muscular legs.

"Right that's fine, thank you," Frank said before leaving.

After he had gone, Gary gave a sigh of relief. *Mmm, piece of cake*, he thought. The only mistake he'd made was the fact that he didn't ask Frank, why he needed to look at his legs.

Chapter 17

"WELL, GARY KENNEDY'S alibi checked out no problem, which is more than can be said for his father's," Frank told Josephine. "He was with two friends from about 8 o'clock in the evening till the early hours of the following morning and his legs were as smooth as a baby's bottom, not a trace of bite marks, so your hunch never paid off. I must admit though, we needed to check him out, if he hadn't got an alibi for that night he would have been a suspect. He understandably hated Mulligan, in fact he said whoever killed him, did them all a favour, and he's doing a language degree, so I don't think he even knew the tutor Paul Ramsey."

"Did you ask him if he knew Sophie Bryan, who was murdered at the eclipse, she was there for a year or so?"

"No, it didn't occur to me," Frank said.

"Oh, well," Josephine sighed.

"There was one small thing that struck me as odd, though it's probably nothing. When I asked to see his legs, he automatically rolled up his trousers, never even questioned why I needed to see them," Frank told her.

"Mmm… you'd have thought he'd have been curious," she agreed.

"It was almost as if he expected me to ask him."

I wonder…? Josephine thought.

"Still, I suppose we will have to carry on talking to people who hated Mulligan, and believe me there's enough of them, up to now no-one has had one good word to say about him."

"Yes, it went off as sweet as a nut. I tried not to sound too calm, after all, I have every reason to want Mulligan dead, and I said as much. The police went to speak to Terry and Mel, and they even looked at my legs, so as you said Jack, they suspect the murderer has bite marks on his leg. I kept calm even when they asked me my whereabouts on the night, and I sounded vague and a bit forgetful, just as you told me." Gary spoke to Jack like as schoolboy who was trying to impress the teacher.

"You did okay Gary, good job I mentioned the dog, still we're not out of the woods yet, two down and one to go."

"I know and it's me that's got to do it," Rob added nervously.

"It can't possibly be any worse than mine, even I didn't allow for some mad dog, and yet I thought I'd got all hiccups covered. The only difference is I want to see the look on Miranda's face, watch her squirm."

"Don't be ridiculous Jack, no way! What about your alibi?"

"I'll be miles away when you kill her."

"I don't understand," Rob told him.

"I thought that if you kidnapped her, I know a derelict house where we can tie her up. I just want to see her and tell her it was me who planned her death, for all that she's done to me, and that I'll never be caught as I'll be miles away when you finish her off. I need to see the panic and terror in her face," Jack said malevolently.

He went through his evil plan with Rob, and Gary listened silently.

"I don't think you ought to see her, let's face it, anything can go wrong," Rob told him. "I mean for one thing, they might find two sets of footprints, you've read up on forensics, they can easily place two people as well as the victim at the scene of crime."

"Mmm... you've got a good point there Rob, perhaps I need to give it more thought. It's just that somehow, I want her to know that it's me who's punishing her for all she's done. Anyway I've got things to do. I'll be in touch with you both later."

After he had gone, Rob turned to Gary.

"I think he's losing it."

"Yet he's been so calm and level-headed up till now. He's got revenge for both of us, and at the same time kept us safe, and out of prison. He's been brilliant, but I don't understand this," Gary added.

"Maybe it's because he's personally involved this time," Rob suggested.

"Yes, but whatever she's done it can't be as bad as Mulligan. I would have loved to have been there when Jack killed him and said, 'This is for my sister and mother, you bastard!' But I knew that would be impossible."

"Yeah but remember I'm the one committing this murder. I don't want him putting me at any unnecessary risk, just because he wants Miranda to squirm over her impending death. It all seems a bit cruel and ruthless to me. I don't know if I can go through with it."

"Look Rob, we can't let him down, after all he's done for us. Our two enemies have been disposed of, and Miranda is still alive, we agreed, and if we didn't carry it through, Jack could turn nasty, drop us in it even."

"He wouldn't do that, he's committed murder as well, remember," Rob replied.

"He hates her so much, if you don't get rid of her, he might be prepared for all three of us to go down."

"Well, we will just have to talk him out of wanting to see her, he's got to see sense."

Two days later, Jack was back to the calm, level-headed cool person he had always been, much to Rob and Gary's relief.

"I know it was a stupid suggestion of mine, to want to see Miranda. I let my emotions and hatred rule the situation, which was unforgiveable," he admitted to Rob and Gary.

"Yeah... Well... don't worry mate, we knew you'd come round to your senses, didn't think for one minute you'd let us down," Rob lied.

"After all, it was you who masterminded this entire plan," Gary praised him.

"Yes and the pièce de resistance is yet to come. Now listen carefully Rob, this is what you've got to do."

Chapter 18

JOSEPHINE AND BILL had just finished work and were having a drink at a local pub, The Smugglers Inn, that was situated on the cliffs at Babbacombe. Many times in the past, they had sat outside on a fine day looking over the bay, trying to fathom out some case or another.

Today it was a cold and bleak day in November, and they were huddled over the roaring log fire. After placing his food order, Bill brought the drinks over to the table where they were sitting.

"I told you, you're welcome to eat with me and Andrew this evening," Josephine told him.

"I don't like to impose, you probably want to be alone."

"We're not a couple of teenagers you know, we've been together two years now."

"Look it's no problem, anyway I've ordered a lamb hot pot now."

Josephine took a gulp of her lager and stretched her hands out to warm them over the fire.

"Do you know Bill, I can't help feeling

there's some connection with these last three murders."

"I don't know how you've worked that one out, and don't dare say it's female intuition because I'm not buying it," he replied.

"Okay, just bear with me on this. Sophie Bryan was an ex-student at Exeter University, Paul Ramsey was a tutor there, and the most recent victim Tony Mulligan, the girl who he killed, her brother Gary Kennedy is studying there."

"Okay so the University is a slight link, but it's so obscure, Sophie Bryan studied fashion, the fashion and design department is a separate annex and at least three miles away from where Ramsey taught. I doubt she knew him. Gary Kennedy doesn't know Ramsey and probably didn't know Sophie Bryan, and anyway it's almost like saying Tony Mulligan's aunt's sister's, husband's friend had a daughter there. The place is huge, I bet your Jessica knows people there. One of the PCs at the station has a daughter who's at Exeter. You are looking for some sort of sinister connection that in my opinion just doesn't exist."

"So you think it's all in my mind?" she asked.

"Look, let's re-cap," Bill began. "Sophie Bryan died on a cliff at the total eclipse in August and she was stabbed to death. Two months later a tutor at Exeter University is found dead, okay someone took his mobile phone and insulin and locked him in the room, then Mulligan has his head battered. The three crimes are so completely different. I know it's frustrating but we haven't got a result yet on our two, but then neither has Frank Blundell up to now."

"Do you think we are losing our touch?" Josephine asked.

"Well I'm not, I don't know about you," Bill said, patting Joan the barmaid's bottom as she placed his hot pot on the table.

"It's a good job I know you, and you're a copper," she said pinching his cheek. "Otherwise I might report you for sexual harassment."

"You wouldn't be the first," Josephine joked.

"Look," he said dipping his crusty bread into the steaming pot, "We just need a break, something will turn up sooner or later."

"You try telling the Chief that," Josephine replied. "He reckons we've spent too much time and manpower on both cases already."

Miranda had stolen the designs that Jack had spent the best part of a year working on, and Jack knew she had no scruples whatsoever about passing work off as her own. He had decided that the best way to get her to meet Rob was for Rob to offer her someone else's work.

He had never told Rob or Gary the other reason why he despised her so much. Miranda was bisexual and not just a lesbian as many people had thought. She had slept with Jack's long-term girlfriend. She never really cared for Zoe, yet she had so much influence and power that Zoe left Jack, saying she now realised she preferred women to men. Even though Jack could discuss most things with his friends, from an egotistic point of view, Jack had always considered himself a bit of a stud where women were concerned. He could never admit to anyone that he had lost his girlfriend to another woman, as his sexual prowess would be doubted.

It was decided that when Rob contacted Miranda, he would say he had some very special exclusive designs, which he would want payment for. Jack knew Miranda wouldn't be able to resist, and at the very least would want to see what Rob had to offer and he was fairly certain she wouldn't mention it to anyone, as they all believed the excellent work she had produced was due to her own talents. He knew Rob had more guts than Gary, whose chain of events for Ramsey's murder had not had even a hint of violence. Then again, Jack had no personal vendetta when it came to Ramsey, as he did with Miranda. Nevertheless, if he planned a death that was too brutal, Rob might have bottled out, or at least asked for something less violent. Rob was the only one to be killing a woman; although in Jack's eyes she was more evil and callous than any man he had ever known, but whether he could include himself in that was debatable. He felt that stabbing Miranda may be too gruesome for Rob, and the amount of blood may be a problem, even if Rob were wearing protective clothing. He wasn't able to obtain the poison he had originally planned to use. He finally decided that Rob should drop one Mogadon sleeping tablet, that had been crushed into a powder, in Miranda's drink, not enough to put her sleep, but just enough to relax her to an extent that it would be easier to get her back to the derelict house.

Jack knew that the job Miranda had landed

at a top design house was in jeopardy. She had only managed to obtained a third in her degree, but it was her designs that had secured her the position, despite the fact there had been several far more talented applicants. The designs that she had shown at the interview were a combination of Jack's, and other talented people she had stolen from, but since she had been working there, the work she had provided herself was not up to standard, it lacked flair and individuality. When it came down to her own ability, she just couldn't hack it.

Jack had given Rob two exclusive collections that he had been working on to entice her, although he only told him to take one or two of the best creations when he met her.

He knew Miranda wouldn't be able to resist them and would want the whole collection at the right price, but obviously Rob would not say how they came to be in his possession.

Rob arranged to meet Miranda at a club that was some miles away. It suited them both, as neither wanted to be seen.

"What I can't fathom out," she began sipping her red wine "Is how you knew I was in the market for this sort of thing."

"I heard it through the grapevine," he replied.

"But look, either you're interested, or not. I haven't come to waste my time or yours."

"Let's see what you've got then."

He carefully opened the folder, and produced two of Jack's designs.

"Mmm…" she said studying them carefully.

He could see by the expression on her face, she was very impressed.

"They're not bad…" she remarked.

"Come off it—they're brilliant and you know it."

"I'll need more," she told him.

"There are two collections with about fifteen designs in each, and believe me they are all of this calibre."

"Okay, so what sort of price are we looking at?"

"Shall we say one thousand?" Rob suggested.

"I couldn't possibly afford that amount."

"Come of it, you're on a good screw."

"The most I can manage is about seven hundred and fifty pounds," she said knowing in her own mind she would pay the full amount if she had to.

"Okay, I need the money desperately," Rob lied.

"What for, have you got a drugs problem?"

"No…" he replied.

"Then why do you want it for then," She asked.

"That's my bloody business, now are you interested or not?"

"Yes, but I want to see the rest."

"Well there's no time like the present, shall we have one more drink?" he suggested.

"Okay, I'll just nip to the ladies."

The plan was going like clockwork, and Rob was able to put the crushed tablet into her glass before she returned.

As they pulled up outside the rather grim looking deserted building, Miranda asked, drowsily, "Is this where you live?"

"No, I can't risk keeping the designs there in case someone sees them," he replied.

"Mmm… I see your point I suppose," she yawned. "God I'm shattered, let's hurry up and see them so I can get home."

He went down to the basement and she followed rather unsteadily. Because the tablet had taken effect she didn't seem worried or sense any danger.

"Can't you put some light on, I can't see a bloody thing."

Just at that moment Rob pushed her to the floor.

"What the hell...?" Miranda uttered.

"Shut up," he shouted as she started to struggle. She was stronger than he had anticipated, even though she had been drugged. She went to strike Rob, and he punched her in the face, rendering her unconscious. He changed into the protective clothing that he had left in the corner of the room, carefully washing his hands in a nearby sink as her nose had bled when he struck her. When he had finally put his gloves on he brought a chair to where she lay and lifted her heavy slumped body on it, and proceeded to tie her up securely. Just as she started to come round, about half an hour or so later, he started to put sticking plaster over her mouth.

"No, please, I can't breathe," she pleaded.

"Okay, but one sound out of you and you're dead—there's no point in shouting as this basement is soundproof," he lied.

He couldn't understand why Jack had told him to tie her up before killing her, he wanted just to get it over with as quickly as possible, still he had promised Jack he would carry out his instructions to the letter.

"What's all this about?" she said. "I agreed on the price you asked, I can get the money tomorrow."

Just at that moment Rob's mobile phone rang.

Shit! Who the hell's that? Why didn't I switch it off? he thought.

He didn't know whether he should answer or not, in case Miranda started screaming for help, so he covered her mouth with the tape before he answered.

"It's Jack," the voice said at the other end.

"For fuck's sake! What are you playing at? I wasn't going to answer, you scared the shit out of me!"

"Is she there?" Jack asked.

"Yes, tied up, just as you said."

"Well, let me speak to her," Jack demanded.

"No, what the hell for?" Rob asked.

"I'll come there then," Jack said.

"Okay, hang on a minute," he said removing the plaster from Miranda's mouth, then he held the phone up to her ear.

"Help me!" she shouted in the phone.

Jack laughed maliciously.

"Hello Miranda, it's Jack here."

"I suppose it's your idea of some sick joke getting me here," she said.

"Good designs, don't you think? But then I was always the one with the talent," he announced.

"So they are yours, I told Rob I'd pay…"

Before she had chance to finish he said, "I knew if I offered you someone's designs you would come like a lamb to the slaughter. Well now, dear Miranda, you're going to die, for all the shit you've put me through."

"They will know it's you, you've threatened me in the past," she told him. "You'll never get away with it!" she said in a terrified voice.

"Oh shut up, I will. I'm miles away and when you die, I'll have the perfect alibi, not that I wouldn't take great pleasure in seeing you face, watching the fear, as you take your last breath, still never mind."

"You're mad!" she screamed.

"Some might say that, others would consider me a genius, for concocting such a brilliant plan. Anyway I'm going now, see you in hell," he laughed dementedly.

She started sobbing and Rob took the phone away from her face.

"For God's sake Jack, you're not making my job any easier."

"I needed to let her know how I felt," Jack explained.

"Well, I felt the same about Ramsey, but I left it to you and Gary."

"Well, I'm going now. I'll see you when it's all over."

Rob put the phone back in his pocket.

"Look Rob, you don't want to take a human life," Miranda pleaded.

"Just shut up. I've got to, I owe him."

"What can you owe him that you need to murder for? Look, I'll give you money, anything, please let me go," she cried. "You'll never be able to live with yourself."

Rob was in a quandary.

Why the hell did he have to phone, everything was going fine up till then?

I don't think I can go through with this... But the other two have done their part... I can't let them down. But can I kill her?

"Rob, please, let me go!" she begged again.

"Yes, and watch you go straight to the police!"

"No I won't, I give you my word."

He walked away and pulled at his hair, his mind was in turmoil.

What the hell shall I do? he thought.

"Look," he began, "he avenged my girlfriend's death for me by getting rid of Ramsey. She was coming off the drugs, we

218

would have had a life together."

"You're not like Jack, he's a devious bastard," she said.

"I'd say you're the one who's devious, pinching all his designs, and passing them off as your own, and you were quite prepared to do it again. So you're not little Miss Perfect."

"Okay so I did take somebody else's work, maybe it's not right, but surely it doesn't deserve the death penalty."

Rob looked confused and unsure, as he started to perspire.

Please God, I hope he's weakening, Miranda thought.

"Look, you don't really want to kill me," she looked pleadingly with big brown eyes. "Tell me what I need to do to save myself."

I just don't know if I can go through with this.

Oh shit Jack, if you hadn't asked me to tie her up just so you could speak to her it would have been over and done with by now.

"Please," Miranda started crying again.

Why couldn't I have dropped cyanide in her drink or something?

"Can't Jack do his own dirty work?" Miranda asked.

"I owe him one, he got rid of Ramsey for me," he disclosed foolishly.

I can't do it, but I've got to, especially since I've told her that.

"Why did you want Ramsey dead?"

"I'd have thought that was obvious, he caused Claire to kill herself when he said she was useless, he constantly put her down. She was coming off drugs, kicking the habit, but his criticism put her back to square one," Rob told her.

"Drug taking's for losers! How do you know she killed herself? Stupid cow probably OD'd. Everyone knows junkies are just waiting to die!"

"Don't say that. You didn't know what Claire was really like, I loved her and she was beating it."

Why the hell did I say that? Miranda thought.

Rob picked up a pair of tights, and stood behind her.

"Look, I didn't mean..."

Suddenly the tights in Rob's hand were around Miranda's neck, there was no time for her to explain or take back what she had said as he pulled tighter. She started to choke and gasp for breath. She struggled to free herself, but she was securely tied. There was just no way she could defend herself.

"How dare you say that about Claire," he

shouted pulling tighter and tighter, "I loved her, I loved her" Miranda's face became blue and contused.

Rob was still pulling on the tights a minute after Miranda had died, repeating the words *I loved her, I loved her*.

He finally loosened his grip, and fell to the floor crying. Not for Miranda, whose life he had just taken, but for Claire.

The anonymous 999 call was made eight hours after Miranda's death, saying there was a woman's body in the basement flat at number sixteen Argyle Street.

When the SOCO team, arrived with the police, and forensics, it didn't take long to identify the corpse, as she had several forms of ID in the handbag that lay near by, along with three hundred pounds in cash.

It was three days later when it came to Josephine's attention, and she realised that the murder victim, Miranda Cresswell, was the girl who was by Sophie Bryan's side when she died.

"Look Bill, there's got to be a connection, although I'm not sure what. It's too much of a coincidence that she's been murdered a matter of weeks after Sophie's death. I'm going to ask the Chief if I can take over the investigation into her murder," Josephine remarked.

"Well you can ask, but I doubt you'll get anywhere with him, we are still investigating Ramsey's murder," Bill replied.

"Someone else can take that over. Look Bill, Miranda was on the spot when Sophie died."

"Yes and so were hundreds of others."

"But she stood next to her, screaming and covered in blood," she added.

"Maybe she knew who had murdered Sophie, is that what you're suggesting?" Bill asked.

"It's possible, let's just surmise she did know the guilty party and was blackmailing the killer, perhaps they had paid out as much as they could afford, and the only option left was to dispose of Miranda."

"Possible, but I'm still not convinced," Bill said rubbing his chin.

"Okay then, let's assume she knew something she didn't know she knew," Josephine began.

"Have you been drinking?" he said teasingly.

"Come on Bill, you know what I mean. Let's say she saw something at the time that she didn't think significant, so it wasn't mentioned in her statement. But let's say the killer might suspect she knows something that could point the finger at him or her, and that eventually it may just click in Miranda's brain, and she'll put two and two together," she explained.

"Okay, let's say I can see what you are getting at, I still don't think you've got enough information one way or the other to convince the Chief. I mean let's face it, it's all pure conjecture. He'll want something more concrete. Anyway if what you say is right, then why has the killer waited all this time before getting rid of Miranda," Bill asked.

"I want to go through all the case notes again with a fine tooth comb and everyone's statement. Maybe there's something we've missed," she told him.

"But you've already re-read them. Don't you remember when you were desperate to find something to tell Sophie's parents…"

"I don't care, we'll go through them again, we need to find something, anything to convince the Chief, that's all I need."

Chapter 19

"I CAN'T SEE WHY you wanted me to phone the police," Rob sounded confused.

"No, I don't suppose you would. Honestly, you and Gary leave everything to me," Jack replied.

"That's because you tell us to. You're supposed to be the brains behind it all."

"Yes I know, but it would be reassuring if you did use your own initiative from time to time," Jack told him. After a moment or so he continued, "Well, can't you work it out for yourself?"

"Was it to do with your alibi?" Rob suggested.

"You're getting there," Jack said sarcastically. Rob still looked confused.

"Since the house was unoccupied, Miranda's body could have lain there days, possibly even weeks, before she was discovered, and then it may have been difficult for the police and forensics to determine a time of death. They could have made a calculated guess, say within a forty-eight hour period, but I needed them to pinpoint her death down to less time, within a matter of hours, so my alibi covered me," he explained.

"I get the picture now."

"Well thank God, it's finally sunk in," Jack said nastily.

Rob became angry. "There's no need to be so bloody sarcastic. You don't know how terrible it was, and you phoning made matters worse."

"Tell me, was she terrified, begging for her life? God I wish I'd been there," Jack smiled, an evil, sick smile.

"She pleaded for her life. In fact, at one stage I though I would weaken, and give in. She asked why you couldn't do your own dirty work."

"Yeah, and what did you say?" Jack was really enjoying hearing the gruesome details.

"I told her I owed you one because of Ramsey," Rob admitted.

"You bloody fool! Look well if she'd have escaped. She'd see to it we all went to prison. I'm amazed you had the guts to do it." Jack became very red in the face.

"Well, if I could have got on with the job, but you bloody phoning, it was like a fucking mother's meeting instead of a murder."

"Still, all's well that end's well, at least you didn't

weaken, you got the job done," Jack stated.

"It was when she started slagging off Claire, that I really snapped, and decided to kill her," Rob admitted.

"So if she hadn't said anything about Claire, it's possible you would have walked away? You pathetic bastard! All three of us would have been banged up because of your incompetence!"

Rob suddenly jumped up and took a swing at Jack, and caught him in the eye. Jack staggered backwards, and fell to the floor. He felt dazed for a few moments as he started to recover slightly and then Rob was on top of him, with his hands around Jack's throat. He managed to twist to one side and knee Rob in the groin. Rob moaned in pain as he loosened his grip on Jack's neck. Jack made his move, pinning Rob to the floor; Rob was in agony, and Jack was tempted to punch him in the face, while he was still down but suddenly he disciplined himself. He stood up and looked down at Rob.

"For fuck's sake Rob, we shouldn't be doing this to one another. We made a pact with Gary. We should be supporting one another, not kicking the shit out of each other. Don't you agree?"

"Yes," Rob murmured weakly.

"Well get up and calm down, I'll do us both a drink."

Jack returned a minute or so later with two whiskies. "Drink this," he ordered pushing the glass into Rob's hand.

"Look we've both been under a lot of stress and strain. Maybe I was too critical," Jack admitted.

"Well, maybe you had a right to be. I realise I should never have told Miranda what I did, but at the time—"

"Look it's all over and done with now. I know the police will come and see me in time, but I've got my alibi all sorted at the hotel in Cornwall, so I reckon everything should turn out all right. We should be proud of what we've achieved," he announced.

"Look, we're mates, and we'll stick together, but there's no way, I'm proud of taking a life," Rob looked at Jack, feeling disappointed at what he had just said. Jack seemed to sense how he was feeling.

"Of course, you're right Rob, it was just a turn of phrase," he lied.

Rob nodded, and drank his whiskey, as Jack looked over at him, thinking.

You're too bloody weak. I reckon even now you could blow it and drop us all in the shit.

228

Josephine sat on her veranda, reading the case notes on Sophie Bryan. It was an exceptionally warm day for November. Although the holiday season was over, there were always pensioners about even at this time of the year, since many hotels in both Babbacombe and Torquay would stay open all year round. Josephine often found she could concentrate better at home as there were no distractions, like her phone constantly ringing and people coming in and out of the department with messages and queries. She slowly went through all the interview notes and statements concerning Sophie's death, and there were quite a few with the families, fellow employees and friends. She paid particular attention to Miranda's in the hope something might come to light. Josephine was convinced that the two murders were linked despite the fact she had nothing definite to support this theory. She had been studying the reports for over an hour and nothing had come to light. She was feeling depressed and disappointed with herself and went into the kitchen to make some tea. As she mooched through the fridge she found a carton of clotted cream that had to be consumed in the next twenty-four hours.

Mmm it's a pity I've got no scones, she thought. So she settled for two digestive biscuits, with a dollop of cream and jam on each one. She carried the tray of tea and biscuits outside.

Maybe if I feed my brain, still any excuse to indulge, she thought.

She held Trudy's statement, the other girl that was present at Sophie's death, in one hand reading it, and the biscuit topped with cream in the other, quickly popping the remainder into her mouth, before a dollop of cream almost dropped onto the paper. It was quite monotonous, until she came to about halfway down the page where Trudy had stated "Sophie was really cold, she had been suffering from flu all week, so Miranda gave Sophie her coat to wear."

Lent Sophie her coat…

Mmm… now I wonder. It was a bright fluorescent shade of lime green that would have stood out even in the darkness of the eclipse. Perhaps I've been barking up the wrong tree, thinking Miranda might have known something about the murder. She could have been the intended victim all along. Her hair was similar to Sophie's, and in the crowds the only way the murderer could determine where their victim stood was by the coat, Josephine thought excitedly. *If the killer didn't see Miranda take the coat off and give it to Sophie, during the eclipse they would just head for the coat, before they*

230

plunged in the knife, and ended up killing the wrong person! Josephine's heart beat faster, as she became more excited.

If that was the case, at some time in the future, the killer would have to try again and this time they had succeeded. That must be it! It's the only feasible explanation. Now all I've got to do is convince Bill and the Chief.

She left her tea and other clotted cream biscuit as she grabbed her handbag and made her way back to the department.

"I can't see why on earth you didn't notice this in the witness's statement before," Chief Cunningham began.

"Well at the time, I doubt if it would have had any consequence. As you know Sir, we had no reason to believe that Sophie was not the intended victim. But, when we could find no motive for her murder, or any suspects, our next line of investigation was that some madman was responsible, and Sophie was chosen at random," Josephine told him.

"I believe," Bill added, "the only reason we couldn't find the culprit, was because she was never the intended victim."

"It's too much of a coincidence, and since

she was wearing Miranda's coat, the killer made a dreadful mistake. It's taken him or her over two months, but I believe they have now got rid of the person they originally intended to," Josephine told the Chief.

"There was a considerable amount of money in her bag, that her killer did not take, why I don't know," Bill said.

"If Miranda had been killed shortly after Sophie's death, it would have looked suspicious and, having failed the first time, it needed to be planned as they couldn't afford a second mistake."

"The deaths are different, one a brutal stabbing and the second being tied up before strangulation, that could point to it being a different murderer," the Chief proposed.

"Maybe the killer wanted us to think that Sophie's murder was a mistake, and that's why we never really got anywhere with the investigations. There was never a needle in the haystack to find," Josephine remarked.

"Okay if I go along with your theory, are you telling me you want to take over Miranda Cresswell's murder investigation?" the Chief asked Josephine.

"Yes Sir, I'm convinced the killer of Sophie and Miranda is the same person."

"Okay, I'll assign you to the case for a month but remember, you still have two unsolved murders, Sophie Bryan's and Ramsey's."

After they had left the Chief's office Bill turned to Josephine, "I can see his point, we've got no results on either case up to now."

"Hey, just whose side are you on?" she asked.

"As if you need to ask that. Come on we've got work to do," Bill replied.

Chapter 20

AS THEY ENTERED the morgue, after donning caps and gowns, Brian Morrison was working on Miranda's body.

"I've heard through the grapevine, you've been assigned to this murder enquiry," he told Josephine.

"Yes, but I had to twist the Chief's arm to get it. Anyway what have you got for me?"

"Because of the anonymous phone call, we were at the scene of crime at eight o'clock in the morning, and as close as I can get I'd say she had been dead for about nine hours. Cause of death was strangulation, as you can see by these pressure marks and bruising," he said pointing to her neck.

"I found traces of Mogadon, the sleeping drug, in her blood, although only a small amount. She may have taken possibly only one or two tablets."

"Or maybe have been given them unknowingly by her killer," Josephine suggested.

"Yes, that's possible, as they had been taken some hours earlier, and they are normally taken just before people retire for the night."

"Would she have been very drowsy or disorientated before she was killed?" Bill asked.

"Not necessarily. There were traces of a small amount of food and alcohol, when I tested her stomach contents. She may have felt lethargic and tired, but I don't believe she was comatose. I should think the fear of knowing she was going to die would have caused the flow of adrenaline to keep her awake. Due to the depth of the marks on her ankles and wrists, I'd say she had been tied up for sometime, before she was killed," Morrison enlightened them.

"Was she tortured beforehand?" Josephine asked.

"I doubt it, there are no other marks on her body to suggest that. There was a bruise on her right knee, but I believe that was caused by a knock some days earlier. Apart from the strangulation marks on her neck and the marks where she was tied up there is nothing to suggest she was physically tortured."

"But possibly mentally, if her killer let her know her impending fate," Josephine suggested.

"Who knows? You'd have to run that one through Andrew, he's the psychologist," Brian Morrison replied.

"I suppose since she was mildly drugged you'd have though her killer would have attempted to strangle her without tying her up," Bill remarked.

"No one can really tell just how the drug affected her. One person could take a sleeping tablet and be out for the count, whereas another individual may only feel slightly tired and relaxed. There are lots of factors to take into consideration, the amount of alcohol and food consumed, body weight etc. all determine how effective a drug can be. Since her hands were tied, there was no way she could defend herself, and the fact that she has no traces of skin or blood beneath her nails supports that."

"So can you give me a picture of possible events?" Josephine asked.

"I'd say she was drowsy when she reached the house where she was found. She may have struggled before she was tied up, but she wouldn't have been too difficult for her assailant to handle. But since she was strangled some time later, I believe she would have been reasonably alert, as the drug would be starting to wear off. Why her assailant waited before he killed her is a bit of a mystery."

"If my hunch is right the person who killed Miranda also murdered Sophie, despite the fact the methods are different. But I find it puzzling as to why she wasn't killed when drugged, it would have made the killer's job a lot easier, as she may have screamed to attract attention," Josephine added.

"But it was such an old building, and they were in the basement, I'd doubt if she'd have been heard," Bill remarked.

"That's all I can tell you at the moment, but I'll contact you if I find anything else," Brian Morrison concluded.

"Thanks, I'll be in touch," she replied.

In the incident room Josephine went through all the details with the team that had been assigned to the latest murder enquiry. She explained that after going through the statements and reports from the Sophie Bryan investigation, the fact that Miranda had lent Sophie her coat, just before she was killed, was significant, since now she had been murdered, it was probable that she could have been the intended victim all along.

"I suppose we should have picked it up at the time," she began.

"Especially when we could find no motive or suspect's for Sophie's murder. So we need to turn her life literally inside out, family, friends, and students at University where she studied her Fashion and Design degree. Once we have a better profile of her as a person, it should help us to find her killer."

The team were split into sections, one of which would speak to the deceased's family, and the others would go to the fashion house, where she had recently started working as a trainee designer. Josephine decided she and Bill should talk to her friends at the university. One or two had completed their degrees in July the same as Miranda, but others were still studying as they had one year remaining.

Her first port of call was the girls that had been present at Sophie's death during the eclipse, Trudy and Sally.

Trudy appeared, a rather mousey looking timid girl who was a year below Miranda and was still at university. She was deeply shocked and upset by the death of her friend.

"First Sophie and now Miranda, it's awful—just awful."

"I know it must be a dreadful shock for you…" Josephine began gently. "Now what I wanted to ask you, Trudy, was that in your statement, you mentioned that Miranda had given Sophie her coat to wear."

"Oh did I? I can't quite remember," she was silent for a few moments and then began.

"Oh yes that's it, Sophie had been suffering from flu, and she said she was cold, so Miranda gave her the jacket she was wearing."

"We believe it's possible that Miranda was the intended victim as, since she was wearing a rather vivid lime green coat, it would have stood out even in the darkness of the eclipse. The murderer could have just been heading for the coat, unaware that Sophie was now wearing it, and not Miranda," she explained.

"Oh... yes... I do see how," Trudy sounded vague and a little dense. "But why should anyone want to kill Miranda... I mean..."

"Well, we couldn't find anyone who wanted to kill Sophie, there was no motive at all that we could see, even though we spoke to ex-boyfriends, family, friends. There was no one she appeared to have upset or crossed," Bill informed her.

"Can you tell us everything you know about Miranda?" Josephine began, "I must be candid, when I say, Trudy, not just the nice things, but if she has ever done anything to you, or anyone else for that matter, we must know. You wouldn't be speaking ill of the dead, and it could help us to find her killer, and possibly Sophie's."

"Yes, I suppose it would, but there's nothing really. I mean Miranda sort of looked after us all. She made arrangements for nights out, advised us what clothes to wear, because she had an eye for that sort of thing, studying fashion. She even told me to drop a boy I was seeing, said he was a loser."

God she certainly had you under her thumb. I doubt you could make a decision to blow your nose without her, Josephine thought.

"So would you say she was the leader of the pack, so to speak?" Bill suggested.

"Well… yes I suppose she was, but Miranda was good to us all."

"Was there anyone she'd upset or argued with recently?"

"Miranda had the odd run in with certain people, but they were usually to blame."

"How do you know that?" Bill asked.

"Because Miranda would always tell us her side of the story."

Josephine felt they were wasting their time with Trudy. In her eyes Miranda had been some sort of Goddess and she knew she wouldn't get a picture of the real Miranda from her.

"Look here's my card," she said winding up the interview, "Please ring us, if there's anything you can think of that will help."

As they left and were just getting into the car Bill said, "That was a waste of time."

"Well, it's obvious she thought Miranda was wonderful, but still, it does tell us what a strong domineering character she was. I formed that opinion of her, when we visited their flat that day after Sophie's death. Although maybe not everyone was as easily taken in and influenced as Trudy."

The interview with Sally was completely different from that with Trudy.

"Miranda always wanted to be queen bee, top dog, and expected everyone to fall in with her plans," she began.

"But you were her friend..." Josephine remarked.

"I could take her or leave her, Trudy was under the thumb, Miranda even made her finish with a decent bloke. I told Trudy at the time she was raving mad, but once the 'Great Miranda' had spoken..."

"So we are all of the opinion she was domineering, but is that a motive to kill?" Bill remarked.

"I had heard that once or twice she had stolen other students' designs and ideas and passed them off as her own. She made believe she was a talented designer, but I don't think she was as clever as she led us all to believe, and let's face it she only ended up getting a third in her degree."

"Yet she landed a job with a top designer," Josephine remarked.

"I know, but how she got it is a mystery to us all, and if she hadn't have been gay, I'd have said she slept with the boss." Josephine looked at Bill, this was something they knew nothing about.

"So Miranda was a lesbian?"

"Well, yes and no, she made out she was, but I believe she was bisexual, I reckon she'd have slept with anyone, if she thought it would have been to her advantage. She used people and then would just discard them, like an old paper bag," Sally explained.

"As you know, she lent Sophie her coat during the eclipse. We believe Miranda was the intended victim, and that the killer made a mistake."

"Yes, that thought did cross my mind at the time," Sally confessed.

"Then why didn't you come forward and say something? We came to a complete dead end with out investigations." Sally looked a little guilty.

"I really don't know. I just though at the time *Why Sophie?* She would never hurt a fly. Whereas Miranda... but I just didn't put two and two together. Then later I just forgot about it... and I was so upset after Sophie's death. It even affected Miranda, she wasn't the same for weeks afterwards."

"Mmm, I wonder if she realised from the start she was meant to be the victim, and was frightened. Still if that was the case why not inform us that she believed her life to be in danger. Unless she was so cocky and sure of herself she decided to deal with it alone," Josephine suggested.

"Maybe it didn't occur to her, I mean did she seem jumpy or nervy to you?" Bill asked Sally.

She thought for a few moments before answering.

"No, looking back, I just think she was genuinely upset. I know she was a cow, but she did think a lot of Sophie even though we hadn't seen her much since she left university."

"Now going back to these designs, do you know who she stole them from?" Josephine enquired.

"No, but the Head of Fashion would probably know, I gather, there was a bit of a hullabaloo at the time."

"Right, thanks Sally. Now, can you think of anyone who would want her dead?"

"Well, plenty of people disliked her, but whether they would have the guts to do something about it, I don't know."

Josephine sat in Bob Jenkins' office; he looked every bit like a Fashion and Design lecturer.

His long hair was tied back in a ponytail and he had an earring in one ear. He wore a rather bright purple shirt, with a silk Mickey Mouse tie. The combination of colours didn't go at all in Josephine's opinion, but someone had once said the worst dressed designers were often the most talented.

"Great pity about Miranda, the girl had a certain talent," he began.

"We were under the impression that in the past she had taken other people's designs."

"Yes... there was an incident, at the beginning of the year," Bob Jenkins disclosed. "Unfortunately nothing was ever proven. If I'd known for certain, she would have been thrown off the course."

"If, as you say, she had a certain talent, then why would she need other people's designs?"

"Fashion design is a difficult career to pursue," he began to explain. "It is very cutthroat, and there are times when people secure positions purely by the connections they have, and not necessarily due to their talent. But saying that, to make a career, you do need that special flair and originality, as the competition is so tough.

"Miranda was a powerful character, possibly that would have helped her make it in a very tough field. Some of our students pursue careers in other areas of fashion, such as say pattern cutting, or as buyers in the fashion trade, but Miranda's ego would never allow her to settle for what, in her eyes, would be second best. It was a designer's job or nothing for her."

"I gather she did fulfil her ambition, and get a position in a fashion house... Millennium Designs..." Josephine said glancing at her pad.

"Yes, she was one of the few to make it."

"Now going back to this incident where some designs were taken, can you tell me in detail what you know?"

"There was a competition, and the winner would be able to show their designs at London Fashion Week. It seems one of my other students Jack Standford, who in my opinion is a controversial, yet extremely talented, student, said Miranda had stolen his designs and passed them off as her own work. Obviously when she was confronted, she denied the allegations."

"Surely when you looked at the work, you'd have known whether it was hers or Jack's. Doesn't each student have his or her own individual style of creating and drawing?" she suggested.

"Well yes, I believe she may have taken his original concept, and altered it to her designs. At the time, there was quite a show down, Jack was throttling her and shouting. 'You scheming bitch'. Even myself and another student couldn't drag him away, so we had to call security."

"Was Jack disciplined for his outbreak of violence, surely the Dean would have had to be notified?"

"Well, to be honest, I didn't mention it. I tried to play the incident down to a certain extent, as Jack may have been expelled."

"So you lied?" Josephine remarked.

"No I just played it down, as I've said Jack is extremely talented, I haven't seen that certain genius in a student for years. I believe he'll go far, I didn't want to ruin his career, it would have been such a waste. Even if he had only been taken off the course for a short time, it would have proved disastrous, as the students need to do a full final collection as well as the written exams."

"Just off the record, what do you believe was the truth of the matter?"

"Unofficially, and just between you and me, I do believe Miranda took his designs. If the same thing had happened to me, when I was a student, I would have probably reacted the same as Jack, in my hot-blooded youth. I didn't like Miranda, and I know others felt the same. After the incident, another student came forward, and said Miranda had almost succeeded in taking some of her work, but luckily the plan had failed and she got nothing."

"Perhaps Jack Stanford should have been more vigilant and guarded his work." Josephine remarked.

When Josephine returned to the department she told Bill of her talk with Bob Jenkins.

"Not short of suspects, then," Bill noticed. "It's just a case of getting the right one."

"I'm more convinced than ever now, she was the intended victim. This Jack Stanford seems a prime suspect, I think we'll pay him a visit," she told Bill.

When the phone call finally came that Jack had been waiting for, he was almost relieved.

Get through this my boy and it'll all be over, and I'll have succeeded with my brilliant plan. Still not quite out of the water yet. Just keep calm and all will be fine, he thought.

Josephine and Bill arrived at his flat the following morning. Jack was very pleasant, and made them coffee. His story was almost identical to that of Bob Jenkins and he openly admitted to them that he would have like to have killed Miranda.

"Can I see some of your designs?" Josephine asked much to Bill's amazement.

Jack went to fetch his portfolio and she took

pleasure in looking through it. She realised just what a talent this young man had, Bob Jenkins was right, he was nothing short of a genius and she praised his work.

"I did a degree in Art, rather longer ago than I'd care to admit, but these are excellent, I'm sure you'll go far."

Bill was getting annoyed, as he felt Josephine was getting away from the matter in hand.

"I know that Miranda Cresswell was far from what some would call a popular person, but I suppose you can see you are a suspect, since you physically attacked her in front of witnesses."

"I know that," Jack replied.

"Can you tell us your whereabouts on Friday nineteenth November, say between 7pm and 1am the following morning."

"Hang on, I think I was in Newquay from Thursday 18th till Sunday."

"Alone?" Bill enquired.

"Well, yes, but I stopped at a guest house."

"That's rather convenient. Why did you go?"

"Just needed to get away to chill out after the pressure of the last year. I've stayed there before and know the people who own it," Jack replied.

"The student grants must be better than I thought," Bill said sarcastically.

"My parents gave me some money, so I used that, anyway, it's cheap at this time of the year."

"We'll need the name and address," Josephine added.

"No problem, I've got a brochure about somewhere."

Jack left the room and returned a few minutes later with a coloured pamphlet in his hand. He gave it to Josephine.

"The Delrene Guest House, St Saviours Road, Newquay," she read out loud.

"Can we take this?"

"Yes, sure."

"If your alibi checks out and the hotel can corroborate your stay, there should be no problem. But can you think if there's anyone else who hated Miranda enough to kill her?"

"Plenty, she was a lesbian, and I know she'd upset several of her lovers, perhaps if you looked into her sexual activity," he suggested.

"A friend of Miranda's, Sophie Bryan, was stabbed to death during the total eclipse, at Berryhead in Brixham. We now believe Miranda was the intended victim," Josephine told him.

Yeah, it was that damn coat, Jack thought. *But how did you work that one out?*

"Apparently Sophie had been wearing Miranda's coat," Bill added almost echoing his thoughts.

"We believe an innocent girl died as a result, as we could find no motive for Sophie's murder."

Fuck... shit... I've got a perfect alibi for Miranda's death, but what about the eclipse? Where the hell shall I say I was? If I ask the others for an alibi they might suspect, Jack's mind was racing, and his heat thumped.

Much to his relief neither Josephine nor Bill asked where he was at the time of the eclipse.

He knew he couldn't tell Gary or Rob that he had killed Sophie, as they would have both turned against him. But he knew it may soon become common knowledge that they believed the two girls were killed by the same person, so he decided to pass on what the police had told him to Rob and Gary.

"So you reckon I'm okay?" Rob began.

"Of course. What are you worried about, after all you never knew her? They will have plenty of other people to investigate. Once my alibi checks out, I'm off the suspect list."

He was just about to say foolishly, *I thought I was the only one whose girlfriend she took*, but he stopped himself, just in time.

"It seems she was a lesbian, well bisexual, they could even be looking for a past lover, so they may have female suspects lined up," he informed them. Rob felt a great sense of relief.

"I'm sorry about the other day," he said to Jack.

"What's that?" Gary asked.

"Just a doubt of confidence, it was nothing," Jack lied.

"The only thing the police did mention, was that, remember the ex-student Sophie Bryan, killed at the eclipse?" Jack began.

"Oh yeah, I read about it," Gary added.

"Well, the police seem to think Miranda was the intended victim, and the girl was killed by mistake, something about a coat."

"Yes, but we know that's not true," Gary stated.

"But just say it was, what a shame, some innocent girl being wiped out. Mind you if it was true, it looks like you weren't the only one who hated her. Perhaps if I hadn't have killed her, someone else would have done it for you," Rob remarked.

That's good, neither of the dumb bastards have even thought for one second, it was me who killed her, Jack thought smugly.

"I've got to hand it to you," Rob said patting him on the shoulder, "it was a brilliant plan!"

"You two talk as if we've done something marvellous, we have murdered three people, that's nothing to boast about," Gary said angrily. "I know that it had to be done, and due to Jack's ingenuity, the plan was carried out successfully, but it's nothing to be proud of."

"Yeah, well yours was easy, it was terrible having to strangle Miranda, and Jack was chased and attacked by a mad dog."

"I know I had the least gruesome some murder, but I couldn't have done it any other way," Gary said.

"Don't you think I knew, that's why I made it easy for you. Rob's right, yours was a piece of cake. I got rid of the bloke responsible for your mother's and sister's death, and nearly got myself killed in the process."

"I'm sorry I was out of order, anyway I've got to go now," Gary said before he left.

"I think he's going to drop us in it you know Rob," Jack said after he had gone. "Something might have to be done."

Rob secretly agreed with Jack. He felt that Gary could be a danger, the weak link in the chain.

"Something might have to be done," *I wonder what he means by that,* he thought. But he hadn't got the guts to ask Jack outright what he meant.

"He's no problem, Jack, I'll speak to him and make sure he knows we have to stick together. I'm certain he won't bring it up again."

"Just make sure he doesn't Rob, because remember, if he turns chicken it's your neck as well as mine," he reminded him.

God, what if Jack has considered disposing of Gary. Maybe he might think the same about me. He seems to have forgotten about our fight but has he? Rob was very frightened.

Josephine was sitting at her desk with Bill when DC Sally James entered. She had been to see the owner of Millennium Designs, where Miranda had worked.

"So what have you got for me?" Josephine asked her.

"It seems Miranda didn't get a good grade in her degree, but the designs she took to her interview were so impressive, they decided to take her on, along with the fact she had her designs shown at London Fashion Week," she enlightened her.

"It's possible the designs she took to her interview weren't her own work."

Sally looked confused, so Josephine went on to explain about her conversation with the tutor, Bob Jenkins, and the fact that on more than one occasion, Miranda had ripped off other people's work.

"Well that sort of makes sense, with what I've found out. Miranda started the job in September; the owner, Ralph Fern, says her work wasn't up to the same standard as her portfolio, which was far superior to anything she had designed while working there."

"That's probably because they were someone else's designs. She must have felt a little desperate. She had landed the job under false pretences, and when it came to it she just couldn't produce the quality of work needed to keep the job," Bill suggested.

"Yes but remember, Miranda was a tough nut. I can't see her allowing herself to be dismissed from her position because she couldn't hack it. She would bluff her way through somehow, maybe try to convince them she was working on something special," Josephine remarked.

"But sooner or later she would have to produce something."

"Well maybe she would do the same as in the past, and try to get hold of someone else's designs," Sally suggested.

"Yes, but remember, she was no longer at university, so how could she get hold of them," Josephine replied.

"Maybe she had contacts," Bill suggested.

"Remember, she had quite a bit of money in her bag, when her body was discovered, we assumed she had been blackmailing the murderer, but she may have been in the market to buy someone's stolen designs. I know it's purely guesswork, but it's possible a hard-up student, maybe on another degree course, got hold of something they knew Miranda would be interested in, they'd sell it just to make ends meet, and maybe it all went wrong. But if that was the case, why the killer didn't take the money is puzzling."

"It could always be a girlfriend she had crossed, who was out for revenge, and we are completely on the wrong tracks, but we need to find out more about her personal life," Josephine added.

"Oh by the way," she turned to Sally "How did DC Barnes get on with her family?"

"From his report, it seems like she didn't have much to do with them. She hardly ever went home, and only contacted them occasionally," she informed her.

"That sounds like Miranda, from the profile we have, though I suppose she would go home at Christmas, even if she stayed here during the summer holidays. I would think they knew very little of her life at university, well, maybe just what she wanted them to know. By the way Bill, have you got the details of Jack Stanford's alibi?"

"Yes, apparently he checked into the hotel in question at ten o'clock the night before Miranda's death."

"Still, it's possibly he could have travelled back, murdered her, and then returned to the hotel," Josephine proposed.

"No go I'm afraid," Bill began.

"According to the owner of the Delrene Guest House, on the night in question he had his evening meal there, and then stayed in the hotel bar playing cards with two of the locals that frequented the place, it seems the hotels open to non residents. He was in the company of at least three people till very late, it would be impossible for him to travel back to Devon."

"I suppose at this time of the year there's hardly any trade, unlike say Torquay which is frequented by visitors, even during the winter months. Parts of Cornwall can be desolate, I suppose it's only from the local trade they are able to survive," Josephine remarked.

"I wonder why Jack Stanford decided to go there in November," Sally said.

"According to the owners, he had been there before in July with friends, they had come for the surfing, as the nearby beach is popular with surfers," Bill informed them.

"I take it he never surfed this time, the sea would have been so cold. Mind you saying that if he had a wet suit, they can be warm. Did the others happen to mention if he'd bought any equipment with him?" she asked Bill.

"Well no, but I could check I suppose, still I can't see what difference it makes." Josephine frowned she looked vexed and deep in thought.

After a few minutes Bill said, "You look odd, what's up?"

"If he didn't surf, why go all the way down there at this time of the year?"

"I'd say lucky for him he did, since he'd threatened Miranda both physically and verbally he'd certainly have been in the running as far as suspects go. Still the only way of finding out why he was there is to ask him. Shall I try and ring him?" Bill asked.

"No I'll go myself, in person," Josephine replied.

Jack was shocked to see Detective Inspector Josephine Blake, so soon after his first interview. For a split second he almost doubted his own movements, even though several people could corroborate them.

Surely… the meal, then… then I played cards with the two old chaps… till way after midnight … it all must fit okay?

Josephine, who was very observant, detected uneasiness in his manner and asked, "Are you okay, Mr Stanford?"

"Oh… yes… just a late night, that's all, effects of the alcohol probably still in the system," he answered, pushing his long black curly hair out of his eyes.

"I'll be okay once I've got some caffeine in my system. Will you join me?"

"Yes, thanks."

A few minutes later he returned with two mugs of coffee, he relaxed for a moment, and then said foolishly "I gather you've come about my alibi."

Damn and blast, why the hell did I say that? Still I can't take it back now, keep calm. He smiled at Josephine as he handed her the coffee.

"Why should you think that?" she asked.

I thought she was the soft touch out of her and that Sergeant she came with, admiring my work, and saying how talented she thought I was. But she's as tough as nails.

"I don't know, can't think why you should want to see me about anything else. I suppose," he answered casually, although his stomach was tied up in knots.

"Mind if I smoke?" he asked. She nodded assent and he lit up.

"Would you?" he pointed the cigarette packet toward her.

"I've given them up," she said.

"Your alibi checks out fine, all the staff remember you, so there's no problem as far as Miranda's murder is concerned, you are in the clear."

"Well, that's nice to know," he sounded relieved, but still felt he wasn't completely out of the woods.

261

"I just wanted to know why you visited the hotel, at this time of the year, I know you went there in the summer."

"Yes, it's excellent for surfing." He walked to a nearby long cupboard and produced a rather brightly painted surfboard, as if he had to prove his point.

"I gather you didn't surf this time?"

"God, no. Far too cold even with a wet suit, and the sea would have been too rough. I'm a bit of an amateur compared to some, I wouldn't have chanced surfing alone."

"Then why did you visit the hotel alone, at this time of the year, and on this particular weekend?"

"I just needed to get away, I find it a peaceful spot, and with all the stress and strain of the exams, I find even just walking along the beach restful and relaxing".

Even though Josephine adored the beach and sea and would spend hours walking along the beach by her house, which she found therapeutic, especially when she was working on a gruesome or stressful case, for some strange reason, she didn't quite believe him, but she didn't know why.

"Well, that's all," she said, finishing her coffee. "How do you think you'll fare with the job situation, when you graduate?"

"Although I've got a few months to do, I've already started to apply for positions, there's one or two in the pipeline. I'll just have to keep my fingers crossed."

"I'm sure you'll be successful, as you are very talented," she told him.

"Unfortunately, so are many others," he stated.

"Well, he checks out one hundred percent, so now I think we ought to concentrate on her personal life. Perhaps the motive lies there since she was bisexual, she could have upset someone of either sex, it may be a crime of passion, sexual jealousy, that's the area I think we ought to explore," Bill said as he sat in the canteen munching his bacon sandwich.

"Yes, I suppose you are right, I'll leave it to you to speak to anyone she was involved with in the past year or so," Josephine replied lethargically.

"You don't sound very enthusiastic," he told her.

"There's something about the last three murders that's bothering me," she told him.

"What's that?"

"I don't know. I can't put my finger on it."

"Perhaps its your hormones, onset of the menopause, your brain's not functioning like it normally does," he remarked.

"Typical male comment and to think I actually thought you were improving Bill. I'd say my brain is working a damn sight better than yours."

"Well, when you actually know what's bothering you let me know," he said shaking the brown sauce on the remainder of this sandwich.

"I don't think I'll bother," Josephine said as she left.

Josephine walked into DI Frank Blundell's department.

"Hi, how are things?" he asked.

"I'm not sure, can I look through the details of the Tony Mulligan murder investigation you're working on?"

"Sure, hang on a minute," he said looking through his files.

"How's the case going?" she asked.

"Well, we did have someone in custody for a day or so. Apparently Mulligan had knocked the bloke's son off his bike, but it had never been officially reported to the police. The man in question, David Heams, has had several run-ins with Mulligan in the past, threatened him, that sort of thing. It looked promising, but when we investigated it further we had nothing to go on, so we had to release him without charge. What about yours?"

"We're still working on Paul Ramsey's case, but I'm convinced the person who murdered Miranda Cresswell is responsible for Sophie Bryan's death. I believe she was killed by mistake, since at the time she was stabbed she was wearing Miranda's coat."

"Well, on the plus side, if and when you do get Miranda's killer you could tie up and solve the two crimes," Frank remarked.

Josephine photocopied some of the case notes Frank had given her, and took them home along with the others. In total she had reports on four murder cases. She went home at three o'clock in the afternoon, quite prepared to work through the night studying them.

She'd been in the house about an hour or so, when the phone rang.

"It's Andrew, I phoned you at the department, but they said you had left for the day."

"I've got some case notes I need to work on."

"Which one?" he asked.

"Would you believe all four murders."

"So I can take it, you won't be cooking tonight."

"I doubt it. What time will you be back?" she asked Andrew.

"I'm tied up, I would think about nine, or thereabouts. We could go for a Chinese," he suggested.

"I doubt I'll be finished by then."

"Whether you're finished or not we're going." She was about to protest, but decided against it.

"Okay, it's a date, but I must get on now, there's a mountain of files to get through," she said before hanging up the phone.

She went through Paul Ramsey's case notes. The only real suspect Rob Morton had been staying with his sister—lucky for him it all checked out—he was miles away. Yet another one who had a cast iron alibi. She still felt that something about the case was not right, and even though Rob Morton was no longer a suspect she decided to look up his sister's details. Her address and telephone number were on the file, so Josephine rang her straight away on the off chance she might be in.

"Hello 69228," she answered.

Josephine could hear children's voices in the background.

"I'm sorry to trouble you Mrs McKenzie, this is DI Blake here from the Torbay Police."

"Yes… what's wrong, is it my husband?" she sounded concerned.

"Oh, no, not at all. Please don't be alarmed it's only a standard enquiry about your brother Robert."

"Has something happened to him?"

"No, he's fine," Josephine assured her.

"Sam leave your sister alone… could you hold on a moment?" Josephine could hear a clattering and banging in the background.

"Go and watch the TV," it went silent for a few moments.

"Right I'm back. I can talk now I've got rid of those two for five minutes."

"I'm sorry I phoned you at tea time," Josephine said, glancing at her watch. She knew how demanding children could be when they returned from school.

"As I said, there's nothing to be alarmed about ,it's about when Rob visited you, when Paul Ramsey was killed."

"Oh yes, good riddance. I'm of the opinion he was responsible for Claire's death."

"I can understand your anger," Josephine replied.

"All I wanted to know was, did Rob visit you often?"

"No, I wish he did. I could never get him to come down, and I'm all the family he's got since our parents split up, I do wish he'd keep in touch and come to see me more often. Although when he did phone, I put him off to start with, because even though I really wanted to see him, I wanted him to visit at the weekend, I'd have had more time to spend with him, what with the children. But he was insistent he came midweek so I agreed. It was good to see him."

"Yes it must have been," Josephine added.

"So there's no problem?" she asked again.

"None whatsoever, Mrs McKenzie, just routine enquiries. I'll let you get back to the children now, thanks for your time."

"No problem... Bye." She hung up the phone.

Mmm. He insisted on coming down on that particular day, couldn't wait for the weekend, almost as if he had to get away. Lucky for him he wasn't there, but still...

Josephine's mind was in turmoil, and despite the hour, she went to the drinks cabinet, and poured herself a brandy. It was almost six o'clock. She picked up the phone and dialled a number.

"DI Blundell here." He answered.

"Oh, Frank I wasn't sure you'd still be working".

"I decided to catch up on some paperwork," he replied.

"Listen, I know the Mulligan murder is your case, but I've got a feeling somehow it could be connected to the other murders. I can't explain why, it's just a hunch. Bill thinks I'm mad, and is blaming it on my hormones."

"Dear old Bill, still a bit of a chauvinist eh?"

"I bet you secretly think the same."

"Not at all. I can remember in the past your strange hunches have turned something up, whether it was relevant to the cases was another matter," he teased. "Seriously though, how can I help?"

"Rob Morton insisted on going to his sister's during the time Ramsey was killed; in a strange way it was as if he almost knew and had to get out of the way."

"Well, Gary Kennedy's alibi checked out no problem."

"Yes I know, I've just been reading his statement, had drinks with friends, then a curry and never left them."

"If it checks out I can't see..." Frank began.

"Listen, I want you to speak to his friends again, and find out whose idea it was to go out, their's or Gary's, and who suggested the curry afterwards."

"Well I will, if you want me to, but I really can't see it's relevant. Whoever's idea it was, it checked out and if he was with them, Gary Kennedy couldn't have been battering Mulligan's head in even if he wanted to."

"Look Frank, just humour me."

"I'll get back to you in a day or so," he told her.

"Thanks, I owe you one."

When Andrew arrived home, he expected Josephine to be surrounded by papers, and making some excuse not to go for the meal. But much to his amazement, she had washed and changed, and put some fresh make-up on, and had a gin and tonic with ice and lemon ready and waiting for him.

"This is a nice surprise, but not what I expected. I though you'd be behind a stack of files."

"Am I really that bad?" she asked.

"Only when you've got your teeth into a case you can't crack," he replied.

"You know Andrew, sometimes it's uncanny, you know me better than I know myself."

"The signs of a good forensic psychologist," he boasted.

"Well, I believe every woman should have a certain amount of intrigue and secrets," she remarked.

"And I'm sure you have your fair share of both. Anyway enough talk," he said downing his drink. "Give me five minutes to change and we're off."

The Chinese meal was delicious. Andrew ordered special fried rice with black bean sauce for himself and Josephine chose duck in plum sauce, with some prawn crackers. They shared a bottle of wine, but didn't order a sweet, as they were full after the meal.

"Do you know, I really enjoyed that," she said pouring the remains of the bottle into their glasses. "I've been going though the case notes for Mulligan's, Ramsey's, Sophie's, and Miranda's murder."

271

"Why all of them? Surely one's Frank's, and you've put the other one on hold? I can't see the point."

"The only real connection is that I firmly believe Miranda's and Sophie's murderer is the same person, but the others seemed connected through the University."

"That's just coincidence, in my opinion," Andrew told her.

"You could be right. Ramsey was a lecturer, and though the original suspect, Rob Morton, worked at a local pub his alibi checked out."

"Well, Tony Mulligan's murder had nothing to do with the university," Andrew continued.

"Yes but Gary Kennedy was a suspect, he's a student there, he had every reason to hate him after what happened to his sister," Josephine told him.

"Yes but so did lots of other people, and he was out with friends at the time of Mulligan's murder, so he's in the clear."

"Then there's Miranda's murder, Jack Stanford again a suspect."

"Yes, but Josephine," Andrew interrupted. "He again had an alibi, he was miles away in Cornwall, so he's not connected.

"Look, your original suspects all had cast-iron alibis, so since they have now been eliminated, you have to look for other suspects."

"I need to discuss something with you," she said.

"Okay, let me get the bill and we'll have a walk along the seafront, I could do with some fresh air, I feel stifled," Andrew said undoing the top button on his shirt.

As they walked along the promenade Josephine began, "Bill thinks it's my hormones, and I'm not thinking things through."

Andrew burst out laughing. "I wouldn't expect Bill to say anything else, but in his defence, Jo, when the card's are down, he's always backed you up."

"I know that," she admitted.

"Look, I've asked Frank to go through Gary's alibi again there are no flaws in it as such, it's just that I need to know if it was his suggestion to go out on the evening of Mulligan's murder."

Andrew was just about to speak but Josephine continued.

"Rob Morton hated Paul Ramsey, threatened him in public, blamed him for Claire's death, and so on, but he had an alibi. He was at his sister's, but he had hardly ever saw her, why suddenly insist on going at that time? She said she tried to put him off till the weekend but he was insistent he came on that day. It's almost as if he knew Ramsey would be murdered, so he had to be out of the way. Then going on to Jack Stanford, again he hated Miranda, he'd threatened her when she'd stolen his work, another prime suspect again miles away at the time of her death, at a hotel in Cornwall."

"Had he been there before?" he asked.

"Yes," she replied.

"There you are then."

"But that was in the summer, not bloody November."

"Then did you ask him why he chose to go at that time?" Andrew asked her.

"Yes, he said he felt stressed, and needed to get to the sea."

"Well Jo, if anyone can relate to that you can, the amount of times you spend just looking out across the water."

"I know that, but it's almost again as if he knew she would be killed and needed to get as far away from the scene as possible."

"Let's just say I can vaguely see what you are getting at, it's an idea, nothing more. It would never stand up in court and if you told the Chief, he would think you'd gone bananas!"

"And I suppose you think the same."

"No, I can see what you are getting at, both prime suspects, both miles away at the time the murders were committed. They had perfect alibis, fate was on their side."

"But was it purely fate, or their own doing, did they make a conscious effect to go away...?"

"I don't think so; let's just take Rob's case, his sister was always asking him to visit, stay in touch, maybe he felt guilty he'd been neglecting her and just decided to go. I can see your idea, but you haven't got enough to go on."

Chapter 21

TWO DAYS LATER, Frank got back to Josephine, with the information she had asked for.

"That was quick, Frank, I didn't expect to hear from you so soon."

"I managed to get hold of the young man in question, a Mr Terry Spiers. It seems Gary organised the evening out, and when they left the pub, he suggested a curry. Terry and the girl Mel were broke and they told him so, but Gary offered to pay," he informed her.

"It was almost as if he needed to be in company during the murder," Josephine told him.

"But there was no way he could possibly know that Tony Mulligan would be beaten to death on that particular evening."

"Yes, but did he?" she asked.

"I'm sorry, you've lost me," Frank looked puzzled.

"Maybe I'm clutching at straws, and it's some mad idea, or I'm desperate for a result, but there's something, I know there's something."

"She's on to us. I tell you," Rob said nervously, as the three of them walked along the cliffs.

"Stop worrying, she's got nothing," Jack said firmly.

"Don't you think it's funny, she phones my sister, and the silly cow tells her she's always asking me to stay but I never accept the invitation. Then out of the blue, I phone her up midweek and ask if I can go."

"So what! It's not a crime to visit your sister. This DI Blake might have a bee in her bonnet, but she can't prove a damn thing. She asked me why I should go down to Newquay in the wintertime, and asked if I intended to surf. I told her it was just to re-charge my batteries, after the exams. I never thought anything of it," Jack told him.

"So how come she needs to know why I visited my sister at that time, and the same with you about the hotel in Newquay?" Rob asked Jack. Before he had time to comment Gary said, "That DI Blundell, who's investigating Mulligan's murder, went to see Terry, and wanted to know if the night out and curry was my idea. It's bloody odd all our alibis have been looked into a second time."

"I agree," Rob said.

"She's getting too close for comfort, I don't mind admitting I'm getting scared."

"If we lose our cool, we'll blow it. She's got nothing. So what if it was Rob's idea to see his sister, and you organised the curry, it's all circumstantial, it would never hold up in court," Jack tied to reassure them.

"Just the fact she's asking all these questions makes me feel she's on to us," Rob said.

"Look, maybe she does think it was a bit convenient, but at the end of the day we were all miles away from the scenes of the crimes, so there's nothing to connect us. Eventually the police will realise they can get nowhere with this line of investigation, and they will go and hound some other poor sod! I know they have been talking to an old girlfriend of Miranda's who was her lover, but they finished, maybe they suspect her. Remember they've got three murders, and no results, maybe their superior is on their backs, and they are desperate. All we have to do is stay calm, and carry on as normal."

"What if forensics find something at Miranda's murder scene?" Rob asked.

"Well you wore protective clothing, and you didn't even know her, so they couldn't possibly link you to her in any way. Look lads, we need to keep our heads. So what if you visited your sister, and Gary suggested the night out. At the time of death, we were all miles away. The worst is over, but I don't think we ought to see one another for the next couple of weeks."

"Okay," Rob and Gary agreed rather reluctantly.

"I've heard they think whoever killed Miranda, also killed that student Sophie Bryan at the eclipse, and that that was a mistake," Gary told them.

"Well if they think it's the same person, that takes the suspicion off me even further. If that's true, it means someone else apart from you wanted Miranda dead," Rob suggested.

"Precisely, I told you she was a bitch, and everyone hated her, there will be plenty of other people, now we've been eliminated."

"Mind you if whoever killed that girl at the eclipse made a mistake, how terrible killing an innocent person," Gary said thoughtfully.

"I know, at least ours deserved to die," Rob agreed.

Bloody good job I never told them. I slipped up the first time I tried to get rid of Miranda, but to think I did consider telling them. They would have crucified me.

"You're quiet," Gary said interrupting Jack's thoughts.

"I was just thinking about what you said, it must have been terrible," he lied.

"I don't think I can stand much more of this" Gary uttered in a frightened voice.

"For God's sake pull yourself together, yours

was the easiest. If you had to do what me and Rob did…" Jack viciously grabbed Gary by the collar of his jacket and became very red in the face.

"I know mine was easy, how could you two do that?" he shuddered.

"Well someone had to do it," Jack snapped.

"You're right, I was out of order. I sort of lost it, I'm fine now, anyway I've got to get back." He walked back down the grassy slope, leaving Jack and Rob standing at the cliff's edge.

After Gary was out of earshot, Jack said to Rob, "I've told you before, he's a liability, he needs sorting out."

Rob was too frightened to ask what Jack meant, but in his heart he knew.

"Look," he said grabbing Jack's arm. "Let me talk to him, I know I can make him see sense. The trouble with Gary is the more aggressive you get, the worse he is, just leave him to me."

"Yeah but can I…?" Jack asked.

"Look, at the start you said that me and Gary had to trust you, and we did, now I'm asking you to trust me. Gary won't drop us in it, if he did it would be all our necks, not just yours. I know I can make him see sense."

"Okay," Jack agreed reluctantly. "But one more outburst like that from him, and I won't be held responsible for my actions."

Jack liked to think he was prepared and level-headed enough to cope with any eventuality, but he was rather taken aback when he received a telephone call from DS Bill Hughes, asking him his whereabouts during the time of the total eclipse in August, the time when Sophie Bryan was murdered. He knew what he was going to say months previously, just in case the situation ever arose, but now the time had actually come and it was so unexpected, he was uneasy and scared.

"If I can remember, all my mates saw the eclipse and then spent the rest of the day in the pub. Unfortunately I was sick in bed with gastric flu, so I missed the whole event," he told him.

"I don't suppose anyone can support your story," Bill remarked.

"Well no, I'm a big boy now, and I don't suppose any of the lads would want to stay in watching me throwing up in the sink for hours on end, or sitting on the loo, when they could be in the pub, can you?"

"No I don't suppose they would," Bill agreed.

Jack didn't want to give him the information about going to the doctor on the campus straightaway, as it might get him thinking it had all been planned. But at the time if he hadn't made a mistake and had succeeded in disposing of

Miranda, as originally intended, he knew they might want to know his whereabouts. But since he'd killed Sophie by mistake, and he didn't even know her, he was never questioned by the police at the time. Beforehand he had purposely booked an appointment to see the doctor, even though he was not sick, complaining of acute sickness and diarrhoea, which would make his spell in bed more believeable.

"From what I've read in the newspapers, I gather you think her murder was a case of mistaken identity," he told them.

"Yes that's correct, it's the assumption we are working on at present," Bill replied.

Miles away for Miranda's death, but no-one to support the fact I was supposedly ill in bed at the time of Sophie's murder, shit, this could be a problem.

"It's happened to us all, had one over the eight the night before did you?" Bill asked.

"No, although it's usually over-indulgence of drink and curries, if I am sick, but it was the proper gastric flu," Jack replied.

"Right that's fine then. We have had to ask all Miranda's friends and associates where they were at the time of the eclipse, we haven't just singled you out," Bill said, as if almost trying to reassure him.

Just as Bill was about to hang up, Jack started speaking, "Listen, I've just thought, I did go to see the doc on campus, a day or so before, and he wrote me a prescription out, I'm not saying it proves I was in bed, but it might prove I was ill."

"Right, thanks I'll make a note of that. Do you have the doctor's telephone number?"

"No, sorry," Jack lied, as he didn't want to appear too prepared, "but the University switchboard might be able to give it to you."

"Right, thanks," Bill said before hanging up.

Bill related his conversation with Jack to Josephine.

"Apparently, he had an upset stomach, and spent the day in bed. No witnesses to back up his story, but I did manage to contact the campus GP, Doctor Freeman. He checked Jack's records and he *did* visit him the day before the eclipse, complaining of sickness and diarrhoea. He prescribed a mixture of kaolin and morphine and told him to rest for the next forty-eight hours."

"I suppose it's possible he could have got out of his sick bed to commit murder, I mean some bugs only last about twenty-four hours."

"I don't think he's involved, I can't see your point," Bill sounded confused.

"If we are looking for the same person for both murders, yes it is possible he killed Sophie by mistake, but we know for a fact he didn't kill Miranda, so it doesn't tie up."

"I don't believe he murdered Sophie, but he could just have pretended he was ill."

"But surely the doctor would know," Bill suggested.

"How many doctors do you know who physically examine you when you visit the surgery?"

"Yes, I see your point," Bill said shrugging his shoulders.

"Mine is writing out a prescription before I've finished telling him what's wrong," continued Josephine.

"But what you are suggesting is he went to the doctor's and he wasn't ill, but if, as you've been trying to convince me for days, it's the same person, it doesn't make sense. Miranda had so many enemies, couldn't it be possible two people were involved?"

"Yes, you may be correct, it's just that something is just not right."

"Yeah we haven't caught a killer yet," Bill joked.

"Oh, you know what I mean. Listen Bill I want you to go to the hotel where Jack Stanford stayed and talk to the people again."

"What for, do you think his name will just disappear off the register or the owners will lose their memory?"

"Just speak to everyone he spoke to while he was there," she told him.

"It would help if I knew what the hell I'm supposed to be looking for!" Bill replied.

Three days later Bill came back to Josephine with the information she had asked for.

"A waste of time in my opinion, still you're the boss. He had a meal in the hotel restaurant on the evening Miranda was murdered, and then went into the bar and played cards all evening with another guest and one of the locals. The only extra bit of information is that he made a telephone call from the hotel on that evening, according to the receptionist on duty. It seems he wanted to use the pay phone in reception, but it was busy and he seemed a little anxious, so he used the phone in his bedroom and the number was registered and charged on his bill, when he settled up. It's a mobile number, I have it here."

"Do you know what time he made the call?" Josephine asked.

"About nine o'clock in the evening."

"That's round about the time of Miranda's

death, according to Brian Morrison."

"Yes but if he was on the phone in a hotel in Newquay, he couldn't have murdered her. Do you want me to ask him who he was calling?"

"No, we'll trace the number and see whose it is. It may be of no consequence, but if we tell him first he may warn the person we intend to contact them."

"I've done a trace ma'am as you requested and the telephone number that Jack Stanford rang from his hotel bedroom was 01197 62531 and is a mobile registered in the name of Mr Robert Morton," DC Barnes told Josephine and Bill.

"Hang on, is it the same Rob Morton we interviewed when Ramsey was murdered?" she asked excitedly.

"Yes, ma'am, the very same," Barnes replied.

"Even though his alibi checked out completely and he's in the clear, it's a turn up for the books, the fact that Stanford rang him," Bill remarked.

"I didn't realise they knew one another, it's odd they have both been suspects in murder cases," Barnes said.

"Neither did we," Josephine began. "They were both involved as far as they were prime suspects who had every reason to want the victims dead, except they were both miles away at the time of death, with cast-iron alibis. So they're in the clear."

"Still what I'd like to know is why was Jack phoning Rob? It could be something or nothing."

"Coincidence though," Josephine added.

"Not really, Rob works at the pub all the students use, Jack drinks there, so maybe they got chatting."

"Okay, I can buy that but why call him from Cornwall on the night of Miranda's murder," Josephine asked.

"I think you are looking for something sinister, that doesn't exist," Bill told her.

"I disagree, somewhere there's a link. How it is connected to the murder, I just don't know. I don't want Stanford to know this information, as it might give him a chance to concoct a story."

"Maybe, he doesn't need to concoct anything, and there's a perfectly reasonable explanation. Still forewarned is forearmed I suppose."

They phoned Rob Morton at the pub where he worked and asked him to come to the station.

"Why, what's wrong?" he asked very alarmed.

"Nothing to worry about, just a minor thing that needs clearing up, we won't keep you, but if it's inconvenient, we can always come to the pub."

"No, I'll take an hour off work and come to see you," he told them. "Will this afternoon be okay?"

"Yes about four o'clock if you can make it."

Shit! I've got to contact Jack.

He rang Jack's phone at the flat, but got no reply, so he tried ringing one or two of Jack's friends, with no luck.

I suppose I'll have to drop a note in his flat. But that might be risky. Where the hell is he? This is bloody ridiculous, we should be able to contact one another in an emergency.

After trying for a further two hours, he knew it was hopeless. He poured himself a drink.

What the hell do they want to see me about… maybe it's nothing… keep calm. He poured himself another drink, before setting out for the police station.

"Stanford, Jack Stanford… his name doesn't ring a bell. Should I know him?" he bluffed.

"Since he telephoned you on your mobile from a hotel in Cornwall on the same evening that Miranda Cresswell was murdered, I believe you do know who he is," Josephine told him.

The stupid bastard! I thought he had phoned me on his mobile or a pay phone. But the fucking hotel room! What the hell were you thinking of Jack? Just because you wanted to speak to Miranda, before I killed her.

A minute or so had passed by and Rob hadn't spoken.

"Do you understand the question?" Bill said sarcastically.

"The name Stanford doesn't ring a bell, but I do know a bloke called Jack, that's why I seemed vague. He comes into the pub now and again. You know how it is, you can't always put a name to the face."

Rob's hands were clammy with sweat, and he wiped them on his jeans.

"Do you mind if I smoke?" he asked.

"Not until we have finished," Josephine replied.

She didn't even want a short pause, in case it gave him time to think up another excuse.

"Now why did he ring you?"

Booze, could I say he wanted cheap booze or a mate was trying to contact him or a girl what girl? They would probably check up on who it was, his thoughts raced.

"Can you answer the question?" Josephine said impatiently.

"Sorry… Er when did you say he phoned me?"

"On the Friday at about nine o'clock," Bill said aggressively.

"Oh yes… I remember now, there's this guy who comes in the pub, works for some design house. Jack wanted his telephone number; something about sending him some designs."

"And did you have it?" Josephine asked.

"No the guy only comes in occasionally."

"Do you know his name?"

"Er… not off hand," Rob suddenly remembered a man who had come in who had a chain of fashion shops in Exeter. "Peter I think, I'm not sure."

"So you didn't give it to Jack Stanford."

"No, as I said, I didn't have it."

"Did you happen to know, Miranda Cresswell, the girl who was found strangled?"

"No I've never met her," Rob lied.

"So she never used the pub where you work?"

"She may have done, I can't remember, we get hundreds of students drinking in there. You can serve twenty people in less than half an hour, and you hardly ever notice their faces."

"Have you spoken to Jack Stanford since he telephoned you?" Josephine asked.

"No… I hardly know him."

"Then how did he get your mobile phone number?"

"I don't know, perhaps a mate or someone who works at the pub gave it him."

"Okay Mr Morton, that's all for now but we'll be in touch," Josephine ended the interview.

Rob almost ran out of the station, like a scared rabbit.

I've got to get hold of Jack before they do.

He had a feeling of terror he'd never experienced before. He waited outside Jack's flat for over an hour in the pouring rain, and at seven o'clock Jack still hadn't returned.

"Do you believe him?" Bill asked Josephine.

"Not a word of it. It was obvious he didn't know what to say. I could see his mind racing, trying desperately to think of something we might believe. I think what he said was the first excuse he could think of," she replied.

"We should really try and contact Jack before Rob does. If the two stories don't match up, we'll know for sure that they're both lying. We can't give them a chance to rehearse what they are going to say." Bill suggested.

"I agree we should try and contact Jack before Rob does, in fact we should have had Rob followed, still it's too late now."

It was almost eight when Jack arrived at his flat.

"Where the hell have you been?" Rob shouted. He looked liked a drowned rat.

"I told you not to come here," Jack began.

"Never mind that, let me in," Rob shouted, he was soaked to the skin and shaking. "Something's happened!"

They went inside and Jack got him a towel from the bathroom. "Here dry your hair, I'll do some coffee."

"No, I need something stronger, and you had better pour one for yourself."

A minute or so later, Jack placed a glass of brandy in front of Rob. He knocked it back in one go.

"Steady on," Jack said.

"Have the police contacted you?" Rob asked him.

"No... not as yet," Jack sounded confused. "Why should they?"

"I'll tell you why, you stupid bastard! I thought you had phoned me on your mobile or a pay phone at the hotel."

"It wasn't working and there was a queue for the phone booth, and I was desperate to talk to the bitch. So I used the one in my room."

"Yeah. Well they traced the number back to me. What the hell were you thinking of? You're normally so careful and meticulous."

"Shit! I just never thought," Jack uttered.

"Well they have had me in for questioning. First they asked me if I knew you, and I sounded vague. Then they dropped it on me like a bombshell, said you had phoned my number about the time Miranda was murdered."

"What did you say?" Jack asked.

"Nothing to start with and if they had eyes in their heads they could see I was stumped. Eventually I said some bloke who used the pub, a designer, had a chain of shops, and you wanted his telephone number, to contact him. I thought of that chap Peter, said you wanted to see if he was interested in your designs."

"Couldn't you think of anything else?" Jack asked.

"No, not on the spur of the moment. I had to concoct a reasonable explanation that made sense. It was a bloody nightmare, in fact I doubt even the great Jack Stanford could have done better."

Jack was silent for a minute or so.

"You did okay, Rob, there was nothing else you could have said. Do you think they bought your story?"

"Your guess is as good as mine. I certainly didn't look relaxed and confident. But I knew I had to get to you before they did so our stories tallied."

"It's a bit of an obstacle, but if we keep our heads, there's nothing they can prove." Jack tried to reassure him.

294

"They asked me if I knew Miranda, if they ask me my whereabouts on the night she died, I'm stumped, I've got no alibi. They also asked me how you got hold of my mobile number, and I said you probably got it from someone at work, or a friend. Anyway do you think we ought to tell Gary?"

"No, he'll only panic, he's not involved in this particular incident, so let's keep it that way."

"I don't think even Gary would have panicked more than I did, I was bloody terrified," Rob admitted.

"Okay, let's get this in perspective, so we know one another and I phoned you, I was still miles away, when she died. There's no reason why they should think for one minute that you killed her. You did well, Rob, if it had been Gary in your shoes I reckon he'd have blurted the whole plan to the police. Look, you had no motive to kill Miranda, you didn't even know her, try not to worry."

"If you hadn't phoned Miranda telling her of her impending fate, none of this would have happened."

"It was bloody stupid of me, I know that, I made a dreadful mistake, but it's a set-back that's all."

"Well I think it's set them on our track," Rob said before he left.

Chapter 22

"WE'VE GOT ALL these odd pieces of information, hunches, and coincidences, if only I could tie them all up. It's like a complicated jigsaw with one or two vital pieces missing," Josephine told Bill.

"Some might say we have nothing at all," Bill added.

"Let's go through it. Jack Stanford had every reason to want Miranda dead, he hated her, threatened her in public and so on. But at the time of her death he was miles away, it wasn't just an alibi, you could call it a perfect alibi. Then Rob hated Ramsey, devastated at his girlfriend's death, attacked him et cetera. Again he was miles away when he died. So he was exonerated from the list of suspects. Now we find these two who conveniently had cast-iron alibis know one another."

"But they may only be acquainted, not partners in crime," Bill suggested.

"Well it was obvious Rob was lying through his teeth. He didn't want us to know the real reason Stanford phoned him. Why was he so nervous and jumpy, if he had nothing to hide? Maybe the two murders are connected."

"In what way? Miranda didn't know Ramsey and vice versa," Bill asked.

"Yes but the prime suspects did," Josephine stated.

"But there's still no case, they would laugh you out of court."

"Look, humour me here. What if Rob disposed of Miranda for Jack, and he did the same with Ramsey and say Jack phoned Rob to see if he had carried out his task successfully."

"If that was the case, it's bloody stupid to use the hotel phone, knowing the number could be traced, and I'm afraid Jack Stanford doesn't strike me as stupid. In fact quite the opposite, I'd say he's clever and devious," Bill remarked.

"He could have slipped up, made a mistake. Anyway while Rob is safely tucked away at his sister's house, Jack carries out the tasks needed to ensure Ramsey's death."

"Yes, but what if Jack was in a lecture at that time? Then that theory would go out of the window... Still we could check his whereabouts, I suppose," Bill replied.

"Look, say I'll murder A for you, if you murder B for me, like Alfred Hitchcock's *Strangers On A Train*," Josephine suggested.

"And what about Mulligan's and Sophie Bryan's death? They don't tie in at all. If your assumption was right, who accidentally killed Sophie at the eclipse?"

"I suppose there's always a chance we were wrong thinking Miranda was the intended victim, and Sophie's murderer is an entirely different person... Oh I don't know. My mind's in a whirl. Anyway we need to talk to Jack Stanford, but I suppose by now, Rob has already contacted him."

"What we should have done, in retrospect, is had them both in at the same time, Rob in one room, and Jack in the other. I bet you a thousand pounds, their stories would have been different," Bill remarked.

Jack rehearsed in detail what Rob had told him, and his story was more or less the same.

"I suppose he's been to tell you what he said," Bill suggested.

"No, I haven't seen him, I hardly know the chap. I just happened to think about the chap with the shops and phoned Rob on his mobile to ask if he had the number."

"And where was he when you phoned," Josephine asked.

"I think he was at home, I could hear the TV in the background."

"So was he able to give you the information?"

"No unfortunately, he hadn't been in the pub for sometime, Rob said he would try and get his address the next time he dropped in for a drink."

"You telephoned him at about the time Miranda Cresswell was killed or at least held captive," Josephine informed him.

"Did I? Well that's neither here nor there, just a coincidence I suppose. Look I'm not involved in her murder, and neither is Rob," he announced.

"We never suggested he was," Josephine replied.

"Well you seem to be putting a lot of emphasis on the time, so I just assumed. I hardly know Rob, and I don't think for one minute he knew Miranda," Jack looked nervous and agitated, even though his voice was calm.

"Well, I think that's all for now," Josephine said standing up.

He looked relieved, "Well, phone me if I can be of further assistance," he said as they left.

"Well, do you believe him?" Josephine

asked Bill on the way back in the car.

"No, it's obvious he's gone through the story with Rob, so he gets it just right, but even if they are lying I don't know why. Let's just say neither of them was involved in Miranda's murder, they don't want us to know what the call was about. Perhaps they are peddling drugs," Bill suggested.

"There's nothing to back that theory up, I don't believe either of them are users, and I'm convinced Rob is very anti-drugs, especially since Claire's death. No, I don't think it's that, Bill. They are hiding something, but I don't know what."

"Now look," Rob said to Gary, "Jack didn't want me to tell you this but…" Gary looked nervous. "The stupid bugger phoned me from his hotel in Cornwall on my mobile, just before I killed Miranda."

"Why, in heaven's name?" Gary asked.

"Because he wanted to speak to her, hear her squirm, beg for mercy, that sort of thing. In fact, if I hadn't have talked him out of it, he wanted to see her in person. Anyway, the point is the police found out, and traced the number back to me. I tell you Gary, it was the closest I've come to having a bloody heart attack, when the police asked me why he'd phoned."

"God, rather you than me! I reckon I'd have cracked up," Gary told him.

"Anyway, I made up some story about this chap who drinks in the pub, who has a string of shops and said Jack phoned me to ask for his number, because he wanted to show him his designs."

"And do you think they bought it?" Gary asked.

"I'm not sure if they believed me or not. If they'd got eyes in their heads, they could see how scared I was. Still, if they did check, the bloke does exist, although I've never actually spoken about it to him. Afterwards, I went straight to Jack's flat and waited ages for him, but I needed to speak to him first, so our stories tallied.

"But the most frightening thing is, what if they asked me my whereabouts on the night Miranda was killed? I could just say I was watching TV in the flat, if they ask the people at the pub, they can't really confirm or deny it. I never came down into the pub for a drink, but no one saw me leave. So Jack's got an alibi, and I haven't."

"But as far as the police are concerned, you didn't know Miranda. Still, you don't think they are on to all three of us, do you?"

"I can't see how they can be, they are suspicious, but I don't quite know what of. We've told the police we don't really know one another as such. They could think, I bumped Miranda off for him, and he returned the favour with Ramsey. But if you think about it Jack was in a class, when you disposed of Ramsey. If they know that, it could clear us in a sense."

"I'm annoyed he didn't want me to know, even though I wasn't involved in this last saga," Gary remarked.

"I think he thought you'd panic. Anyway, they haven't linked you with me or Jack."

"God, if you or me had done something as stupid as phoning, he'd have hung us out to dry. I thought Jack had more sense. It's obvious his hatred for Miranda got the better of him. I'm scared Rob, I think we're all gonna get caught."

"Look, if anyone should be scared it's me and Jack. You are not implicated at all, just keep your head and stay calm, and don't tell Jack I've mentioned this to you," he said tensely.

"You sound as if you're frightened of him," Gary noticed.

"Yeah, well maybe I am."

DC Barnes entered Josephine's office.

"How's the surveillance going," she asked him.

"Nothing much on Jack Stanford, he's just been going about his studies, having the odd drink, but he hasn't been near the pub where Rob Morton works. Whereas Morton has visited the building where Gary Kennedy has a bed-sit, spent half an hour there and left."

"He didn't notice that he was being followed?" she asked.

"No ma'am, I went in plain clothes and used my motorbike."

"That's good," she stated.

She thought for a few moments. "I'd bet my pay cheque on the fact it was Gary Kennedy's flat he visited, and if I'm right that's very interesting. Tony Mulligan killed his sister in a hit and run, but he again had an alibi, the plot thickens!"

Just at that moment, Bill came in, and she told him what DC Barnes had discovered.

"These three are connected," she announced.

"Yes, but only as far as they were all suspects, but they all had alibi's," Bill added.

"Maybe it's some sort of a pact, and they are helping each other out," she suggested.

"Oh no, is it this Alfred Hitchcock's *Strangers On A Train*, theory 'I kill your wife if you kill mine'," Bill said teasingly.

"Yes… no… oh I don't know," she sounded vexed.

"The fact they know one another may be irrelevant. Most people at university are acquainted or perhaps know of a certain person by sight, without ever speaking to them. I mean Tony Mulligan had loads of enemies according to DI Frank Blundell. He said Gary hated him, but who wouldn't if their sister had been killed. Anyway according to Frank, Gary seemed the type to hate violence, and if his assumption is correct, I doubt he'd be in a conspiracy to murder," Bill remarked.

"Well, there was no violence in Ramsey's death, just a case of removing items, and locking a door," Josephine reminded him.

"It sounds good, and would probably make a great story, but in real life I can't see it tying up, and let's face it we have no concrete evidence," Bill replied.

"I reckon Frank could take his pick of suspects in Mulligan's case, and he said Gary had no bite marks on his leg.

"Mind you, we know he wasn't there, as his alibi checks out. We haven't examined Jack's or Rob's legs… but the bite marks might have faded by now anyway. I reckon the only thing to do is have each one in the station individually, sooner or later one of them might crack."

"I doubt it," Bill began. "If your theory is right, it wouldn't be a case of just dropping a mate in it, they would all go down."

"There's always a weak link in every chain," she replied.

"That's if there's any chain in the first place, Josephine," Bill said before leaving.

Josephine went through her idea with Frank Blundell.

"They could be connected, but we now do have a suspect for Mulligan's murder," he began. "Alfred Weeks. Mulligan had been sleeping with his wife, and they had rowed a few days before his death."

"Can you put him at the scene of the crime?" Josephine asked.

"Not forensically, so to speak, but he does have bite marks on his leg."

"That sounds promising. Does he have an explanation for them?" she enquired.

"He's done some breaking and entering, said some dog attacked him at his last burglary," Frank replied.

"God, he sounds a charming character!" she said tongue in cheek.

"All of Mulligan's friends and acquaintances are a rough lot. We are looking into his story and he's had to give us a list of his past jobs, so we've got him on burglary at least and hopefully murder."

"Even if he's not the murderer, he will have to give the stolen goods back," Josephine remarked.

"From what I can tell, he's sold them, but he seems that bloody terrified he might go down for murder, he's spilling the beans on all his past jobs. Still, the case is by no means cut and dried."

"Well, let's assume he is guilty and I can exclude Gary Kennedy. The other two, Morton and Stanford, are far from snowy white, there's something going on."

"Yes, but it may not be murder," Frank replied.

"I'm bloody scared, I can tell you that," Gary said, shaking.

"Why?" Jack asked.

"How can you ask me that? They have tied you and Rob up together and it's only a matter of time before they link me."

"I knew you'd panic, that's why I told Rob not to say anything, but he had to open his bloody big mouth."

"We are supposed to be in this together, I had every right to know," Gary shouted grabbing hold of Jack's coat.

He looked angry and menacing; Jack had never seen him like this before, not even after Mulligan had killed his sister.

"Look, the only reason I didn't say anything was because I thought in this particular instance, the least you knew the better it would be if the police spoke to you." Gary loosened his grip, and Jack walked away.

"We are all gonna hang!"

"Hadn't you heard they abolished it," Jack mocked.

"You know what I mean. This was all your idea from the start, so smart arse, think of a way to get us off the hook!"

"We are not on the hook, they've got

nothing on us. I'll admit she's a clever bitch that DI Blake, but it's all in her mind, she'll never be able prove it, and she knows it!"

"Yes, but she could hassle us for months!" Gary said.

"I doubt it, sooner or later the police funds and manpower will run out. Their superiors will say they have overspent on the amount allocated for the case with no results…"

"Well if you don't do something I'll spill the beans!" Gary told him.

"Yeah and go down with the rest of us."

"I didn't batter anyone to death or strangle them, I might only get manslaughter."

"You'd fucking drop us in it!" Jack screamed as he put his hands round Gary's neck.

"Yours was easy, because I knew you hadn't got the guts for anything else. There's no way Rob and me are going down because of your big mouth. I'd kill you first!"

Despite his violent outburst a few moments earlier, Gary was now frightened. He had no illusions that this was just an idle threat.

"I'm sorry Jack I just panicked. I didn't mean a word of what I said, I'd never drop you in it, I'm just as guilty."

"How do I know you aren't just saying that now to save your skin?" Jack asked.

"Look dad's lost Isabella and mum, the last thing he wants is me locked away, I'd never say anything, for his sake. You avenged their deaths for me by killing Mulligan, and I will always be in your debt."

The furious expression on Jack's face disappeared, much to Gary's relief.

"Look, keep calm. Do you trust me?"

"Yes… I suppose," Gary lied.

"Well, when I tell you they have got nothing to go on I mean it. Of course I was worried when the police discovered I'd phoned Rob, it was a stupid thing for me to do. But when I'd calmed down and thought it through, I knew they had nothing to go on. If we all keep our heads, we'll get through this, I promise you."

"Okay, you've never let us down before," Gary agreed.

"Look, go away for a few days," Jack suggested.

"Mmm, that's an idea, I might stay with Dad, he says I don't visit enough."

"Right, that's settled, go to your dad's and relax, and when you get back it will all be sorted."

Because Gary believed he might be in danger from Jack he agreed to his proposal, but he didn't trust him, and still thought all three of them were at risk of being caught. He told Rob how Jack had threatened him the next time they met.

"Well, I'm not surprised if you said you'd expose us all. It was terrible what I had to do to Miranda, especially when she pleaded for her life. Yours was so easy."

"Do you think Jack will come after me?"

"Don't be silly Gary, he only said that in the heat of the moment," Rob assured him, even though he wasn't that convinced either of them were safe.

Jack was trying to work on his portfolio, but his designs understandably were not up to his usual standard.

I shouldn't have lost my temper with Gary. I'm as scared as he is, but I'd never admit it to him or Rob, one of us has to keep our heads. Still a spell at his dad's house will do him good and when he returns we'll all get together, and decide what we'll say if the police call us in again for questioning.

Chapter 23

A WEEK LATER Gary had returned from his father's house. He sat in the pub getting slowly drunk. He'd already consumed four pints, and it was only eight o'clock in the evening, when he decided to start on gin and tonics for a change. He was trying to chat up two girls, something that was out of character for Gary. But then again he'd never been this drunk or stressed before.

"I suppose you think I'm an ordinary guy!" he mumbled incoherently. "But there are hidden depths to me, if only you knew." He downed his third gin and tonic in one go.

"Knew what?" one girl said laughing.

"Well, that would be telling." He got up from the table rather too quickly, and lost his balance. He staggered into a nearby table and knocked the drinks on the floor before he collapsed.

The barman came over and pulled him up. "I think you've had enough son, time to go home," he took him to the exit, and pushed him outside.

Gary was about to protest, but didn't have the strength. As he went outside the fresh air struck him like a thunderbolt, as he staggered across the pub car park. He walked unsteadily along the pavement for a few yards, before stepping out into the road. A speeding car came out of nowhere towards him and struck him with such force that it sent him hurtling into the air. As his injured body crashed back down on to the road the driver sped away without stopping.

Gary's crushed and shattered body lay in the road, as his life-blood gushed out.

A young couple had just left the pub and were walking along the pavement as a car sped past them.

"What's that in the road?" the girl asked her boyfriend.

"Oh my God, I think someone's been hit by a car! Quick! Use your mobile to phone for an ambulance," he shouted.

"Shit, I've got no credits left, I'll run back to the pub, you stay with him," she shouted as she ran off.

"I could have done with you earlier," the boss told Rob as he came down from his flat. "Some lad from the university was as pissed as a newt; I had to throw him out. I think it was Gary."

Oh bloody hell! Rob thought.

314

"Shouting his mouth off, even knocked a table of drinks over, before I managed to get him outside."

I suppose I ought to go after him.

Just at that moment a young women came dashing into the pub.

"Quick phone an ambulance! Someone's just been hit by a car I think, he's in a bad way! It looks like a hit and run! My boyfriend's with him now!"

Rob ran out along the road, his worst fears were confirmed when he saw Gary's crumpled body lying in the road.

"The car never stopped, do you think it saw him?" the girl uttered.

You fucking bastard Jack. How could you do this?

When the paramedics arrived, Rob went in the ambulance with Gary.

"Do you think he'll make it?" he asked.

"Well at least we've got him breathing again, but he's in a bad way. It's up to the doctors now," the paramedic replied.

After he'd been waiting in the hospital corridor for about an hour or so, a doctor came up to him, "Are you family?"

"No, just a friend."

"Who's his next of kin?"

"His father, but I don't have his address. I

think Gary might have it in his wallet," Rob told him.

"Right I'll go and check his belongings, I'd like his father here before we lose him."

"Can I see him, please? We're close friends."

"I think that will be okay, were you with him when the accident happened?"

"No I'm afraid not," Rob answered.

"His injuries are so severe, I'm afraid we cannot operate."

"Is he conscious?"

"Barely... I'll take you to him," he followed the doctor and entered a room further down the corridor.

Gary's once handsome face was a mass of cuts and bruises and he was hardly recognisable; he was connected up to several monitors.

Rob sat close to him. "Gary, it's me Rob can you hear me?"

Gary couldn't speak although his eyes were open; he seemed to nod.

"Did Jack do this? Tell me. Did you see the car?" Gary didn't answer.

"If it was I'll get him, I promise you that. Was it Jack?"

Gary's eyes closed slowly and the monitor started bleeping. Suddenly two nurses and a doctor pushed Rob out of the way and tried in vain to resuscitate Gary.

Rob sat outside in the corridor and after a few minutes had passed the doctor came out.

"I'm afraid we've lost your friend," he told him. Rob started to cry and in between his sobs kept saying, "I'm going to kill you Jack, I'm going to kill you."

As he left the hospital grounds it started to rain; he made his way to Jack's flat, it was about eleven thirty by this time. He hammered on Jack's door but got no reply.

"Answer the fucking door, you murdering bastard!" he shouted. Fifteen minutes later he was still punching the door with his fist. He knew Jack must be out, because he would have answered so as not to disturb the neighbours.

He walked around all night, he was wet, tired and devastated, when he reached the police station the following morning.

He slumped down on a chair and said to the desk Sergeant on duty, "I need to speak to DI Blake, she's at the Torbay Police Department."

They managed to contact her at home.

"There's a young man here by the name of Rob Morton, ma'am, he said he needs to speak to you, and he seems in a bit of a state."

"Can you get him down from Exeter to our department?" she asked.

"Yes ma'am we have a squad car and two officers available."

"Right thanks, I'll be there in about fifteen minutes, I'll wait for them," she replied.

As he entered her department with a blanket around his shoulders, he looked wrecked.

"Come in here where it's warm. Can you get him a hot drink?" she asked the DC on duty.

As he held the steaming mug of tea in his hands Rob said, "I've got a story to tell you."

How the hell could Jack be so callous and plough him down and leave him to die, just like that animal Mulligan did to his sister, he thought.

"Before I begin, I need to tell you. I know who ran Gary down, it was Jack Stanford, he ploughed him down, in cold blood."

Bill was just about to tell Rob, that they had arrested the driver and occupants of the car, three sixteen-year-old joy riders, who had stolen the car some hours previously.

Josephine looked over at Bill and shook her head slightly, warning him not to give that

318

information to Rob.

"Why do you think Jack killed him?" she asked.

"To keep him quiet of course... this is how it all began."

Rob told them everything as it occurred from the beginning, and how they had carried out the murders. This statement was recorded on tape.

When he had finished and signed a written statement Josephine said, "There's just one thing you said that isn't correct."

"Oh, what's that?" he asked.

"Jack didn't kill Gary in his car. We've got the youths responsible for his death, they were joy riding in a stolen vehicle."

"Oh... Hell, no!" Rob uttered as he put his head in his hands.

"So Jack was innocent, and I've dropped him in it," he stated.

"I wouldn't say Jack was innocent, he instigated two murders, and battered Tony Mulligan's head to a pulp, and we also believe he murdered a completely innocent girl by mistake, Sophie Bryan."

Rob looked confused.

"He originally intended to stab Miranda to death at the total eclipse in August, but she had lent her bright lime green coat to Sophie. Consequently, he murdered her by mistake. So he knew at some time in the future he would have to dispose of Miranda, but his clever plan meant you did it for him, in exchange for Ramsey's death."

"God, how could he have lived with himself, after he had taken the life of an innocent girl who'd never done him any harm?" Rob asked.

"Because he's far more devious and evil than you give him credit for," Bill replied.

"But he didn't kill Gary, and I thought he had, if I hadn't have spilled the beans you would never have proven it. All we had to do was keep calm and I blew it. I deserve to go to prison!"

They arrested Jack Stanford, and brought him into the station.

"I'd like you to roll up your trouser legs," Josephine told him.

As he did so, she noticed the bite marks on his left leg; they were faint but still apparent.

"I'm arresting you for the murder of Tony Mulligan and Sophie Bryan. You do not have to say anything, but anything you do say will be taken down and may be used in evidence against you," she stated.

"I don't know what the hell you're talking about."

"I'm afraid we have a full statement from a friend," she told him.

"I knew Gary couldn't keep his bloody big mouth shut, where the hell is he?" he shouted.

"I'm afraid he's dead," she informed him.

"What!" Jack said shocked.

"He was killed by a hit and run driver two days ago."

"So who the hell...?"

"Rob Morton gave us a statement of the entire plan, we know all about the three murders and how they were carried out," she enlightened him.

"I don't believe it, Rob would never spill the beans, you are making this all up, you devious cow! I'm not saying a word till I've spoken to my solicitor."

A few days later Rob asked to see Jack and Josephine agreed, but they had to be kept several feet apart and be restrained by police officers.

As they both met in the room, Rob began.

"I'm sorry mate, I lost my nerve. It was just seeing Gary's shattered and bloody body lying there dying. I thought you had killed him. It was the biggest mistake of my life," Rob confessed.

"Don't worry, Rob I've made my fair share of mistakes in the past," Jack said thinking of Sophie Bryan. "But you know I'd never hurt a friend. I know I lost my rag from time to time, but I'd never have harmed you or Gary. I'd have died first. We were mates and in it together, no matter what the consequences, I wouldn't let you down. Honour amongst thieves and all that, or should I say murderers! Take care of yourself," Jack smiled at him.

"And you Jack," Rob replied.

Epilogue

"DO YOU THINK we'd ever have cracked it, if Rob hadn't come forward?" Bill asked Josephine.

"I knew they were in some devious pact, but I just couldn't fit it all together," she replied.

"Well, Jack did have the bite marks on his leg, so we may have got a conviction for Mulligan's murder on that alone. But would there have been enough concrete evidence to stand up in court?" Bill remarked.

"Mind you, with Jack's statement about Sophie Bryan's death, we've tied up all four murder cases, although we never really solved them."

"Don't let's be too hard on ourselves Josephine, three people committing three separate murders, not the easiest case to crack."

"Unless all three characters had been very strong and dominant, and then it probably wouldn't have worked. There always needs to be a leader, and there's always a weak link in the chain. Even the best laid plans…" Josephine sighed.

The End

If you have enjoyed this book you will be certain to enjoy these other titles by Janet Harward

THE TEDDY BEAR
MURDERS

Detective Inspector Josephine Blake and her team are on the track of a pyschopathic serial killer who leaves a teddy bear at the scene of the crime.

With her family life in turmoil Josephine tries to outwit the sadistic killer, as Devon is gripped in a vice of terror and mayhem.

"In the best of traditions we are kept guessing to the end."

—*Herald Express*

"A traditional whodunnit with plenty of red herrings and crooked twists."

—*Birmingham Evening Mail*

AVAILABLE AT ALL GOOD
BOOKSHOPS

IN MEMORY OF
MURDER

A tranquil Spanish church is thrown into chaos when Andrew Markham's face and hair become a blazing mass of flames and molten wax…

In Devon, Detective Inspector Josephine blake and her team are searching for a perverted serial killer, as young girls are being held hostage for days, enduring horrible torture before being murdered…

Meanwhile across the country members of the literary establishment are dying in what seem to be a series of gruesome accidents…

Can these events possibly be related?

"The plot is gripping to the end, with Blake under scrutiny from those above her, who doubt that the roles of woman and copper can be combined"

— *Crime Time*

AVAILABLE AT ALL GOOD
BOOKSHOPS

IN MEMORY OF

MURDER

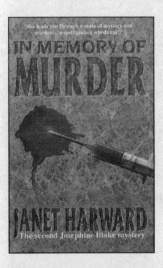

IN THE EVENT YOU
FIND IT DIFFICULT
TO OBTAIN THIS
TITLE YOU CAN
ORDER IT DIRECT
FROM THE
PUBLISHERS AT THE
ADDRESS BELOW.
ENCLOSE £4.99 PER
BOOK (P&P FREE).

*PLEASE MAKE CHEQUES PAYABLE
TO J O'NEILL*

O'NEILL PUBLISHING

34 ROMFORD CLOSE, SHELDON,
BIRMINGHAM B26 3TR

ECHOES OF
DEATH

Investigating a series of horrific murders in the quiet Devon town of Torquay, Detective Inspector Josephine Blake becomes convinced that the killer is deliberately imitating the crimes of one of the earliest serial killers—Jack The Ripper!

When the killer starts to taunt her by email, and threatens the lives of her family, her investigation becomes a terrifying battle of wits that will tax the fall extent of Josephine's resources to their limit.

As the killings continue it becomes clear that the killer may have a specific person in mind for his final victim...

—Josephine!

'A brilliant murder mystery—the book grips and excites to the last twist!'
'A riveting and ingenious plot!'
'Her best yet!'

AVAILABLE AT ALL GOOD
BOOKSHOPS

DEATH
IS THE ISSUE

'Gripping and perplexing, Harward has written a near
masterpiece of traditional crime fiction.'
—CRIME TIME

After a close brush with death Detective Inspector
Josephine Blake requests a six month transfer. She is relo-
cated from Devon to the Midlands Major Crime Investigation Unit in Birmingham. Josephine spent her youth in the
city, but it has changed considerably since then, and she is
plagued by flashbacks to the 1960s when things were so
different for the city and herself.

When a body is found in a sunken narrowboat in a dis-
used arm of the canal system, hidden for five years, Josephine
is seconded to what at first looks like a routine case. Then a
series of mutilated bodies, with injuries identical to those of
the older body are found along the canal system at the multi-
million pound Brindleyplace development. Obviously not
good for the tourist trade!

The victims are members of the city's homeless commu-
nity and identification is a major problem. Josephine liaises
with a private investigator when one of his clients becomes
a victim-could this possibly be the first break in the case?

Plunged into one of her most perplexing and bizarre
cases, has Josephine the grit and determination to succeed?

PERFECT
ALIBI

IN THE EVENT YOU FIND IT DIFFICULT
TO OBTAIN EXTRA COPIES OF THIS
TITLE YOU CAN ORDER IT DIRECT
FROM THE PUBLISHERS AT THE
ADDRESS BELOW. ENCLOSE £5.99 PER
BOOK (P&P FREE).

*PLEASE MAKE CHEQUES PAYABLE
TO J O'NEILL*

O'NEILL PUBLISHING

34 ROMFORD CLOSE,
SHELDON, BIRMINGHAM
B26 3TR